The Adventures of Anzor,

The Adventures of Anzor,

THE STORY OF A HORSE & HIS SURREAL MEDITATIONS ON LIFE, DEATH & PEOPLE!

Pam Maxwell

Copyright © 2017 by Pam Maxwell.

ISBN: Softcover   978-1-5434-5275-4
              eBook   978-1-5434-5276-1

All rights reserved. No part of this book may be reproduced or transmitted in any form or by any means, electronic or mechanical, including photocopying, recording, or by any information storage and retrieval system, without permission in writing from the copyright owner.

This is a work of fiction. Names, characters, places and incidents either are the product of the author's imagination or are used fictitiously, and any resemblance to any actual persons, living or dead, events, or locales is entirely coincidental.

Any people depicted in stock imagery provided by Thinkstock are models, and such images are being used for illustrative purposes only.
Certain stock imagery © Thinkstock.

Print information available on the last page.

Rev. date: 09/20/2017

To order additional copies of this book, contact:
Xlibris
1-888-795-4274
www.Xlibris.com
Orders@Xlibris.com
767427

Introduction

The setting of this story is in England, in an area that really does exist. It is called the New Forest. There, on miles and miles of beautiful woodland and open grassland, herds of wild ponies live. They are an old native breed, called New Forest ponies. Some of these ponies become fairly tame and wander through the villages looking for food.

Glossary

muck out - remove horse droppings

plaited - braided

horse box - a vehicle for transporting horses

hack - trail ride

French meat market - horses were exported to France

Highland pony - a native breed from Scotland

Tarmac-pavement

Note

Spelling is mostly British format.
Both USA &UK styles are acceptable.

Chapter One

I was born at a small riding stable where I lived happily for the first year of my life, with my mother, "Shadow." She was a beautiful chestnut horse, half Arab and half New Forest. My father, whom I'd never met, was apparently a strong bay hunter.

I heard many tales of life in the "big, bad world," but, of course, took no notice. As far as I was concerned, life had begun; with sups of milk, delicious warm milk, and continued with luscious, green grass and crunchy feeds.

Yes, I was totally taken by surprise when the big change came.

It all started one rainy day, as I stood dreaming, grazing at my reflection in a puddle. I was startled back to reality by the strange noises in the tack room. There, Jane, the groom, and George, the stable hand, were making unhappy sounds, their voices strained.

"What on earth is happening?" I wondered. Jane soon answered my question, for just then she walked towards me, flung her arms round my neck and told me the whole sad story.

"Oh Anzor, dear Anzor, you poor little colt, you're going to be sold" Jane sobbed. "The riding stable's closing down. You're all being sold and Shadow's been bought already, though they can't take her for three weeks. Oh Anzor, you'll have to leave us and leave your mother forever. Where will you go? I'll miss you so much, and what will I do?"

She burst into floods of tears. Of course, I did not fully understand. I felt an aching in my heart as her tears silently trickled down my cheek, to my chin. I watched them drip into the puddle, blurring my reflection. I looked up at Jane, her eyes looked like the puddle. I closed my eyes and tried to see the future, all I saw was a grey mist.

The days that followed were very unsettling. Flash, Midget and the big brown horse that I had never spoken to, were all taken away separately, in small horse-trailers. I hoped they had gone to good homes. I felt very insecure and a little scared, for I did not want to be taken away from the home that I loved. I could not really believe for one second even that I would have to leave my mother. I had never known life without her. It was as if she was a part of me. Whenever I was cold or a little scared, I would snuggle close to her. I found myself doing this much more often now.

The dreaded day came. Early one morning, I woke up to a rumbling noise. Raising my head, I was dazzled by the two bright headlights of the horse box, which was to take me far from Dewonberry stables.

As my eyes became used to the darkness, my sight got clear, I could see what was happening. These large horse-boxes had been in the stable-yard before. They had taken the horses and ponies to Gymkhanas. When they had returned, there was always much laughter and often, such good spirits had led to extra feeds. My hopes leapt, perhaps they were going to a Horse Show. My hopes dived to the depths of my hooves as I snorted in disgust at myself, for I knew that was not true.

Shadow whinnied as George approached. I did not struggle as the halter was slipped over my head. I trusted George. Now why had George not spoken and walked away leaving me tied to the gate?

Five of the stable horses were led into the box. Fireworks, the skewbald with the hogged mane, lived up to his name and put on a grand display. He did not want to go into the box. All sturdy 13.2 h.h. of him fought like mad to get away. He reared and screamed and lashed out with his hind legs, once succeeding in hitting the driver's leg. This rough, coarse man, hit back with the big stick he was waving in the air. Poor George did not know what to do. He did not want the pony hit, but knew he had to go in the box. I trembled in pity for my friend. Fireworks was a sensible pony, he must have his reasons for not wanting to go. I decided that the men wanted to take him to some terrible place.

Eventually the pony was chased up the ramp and tied tightly. The battle over and his spirit broken, I saw hate in Firework's eyes. He had never let man near him until eighteen months old. Until then, he had roamed free in the New Forest. He said he was not a pure bred, because some stallion whose breed he had never found out, had escaped from a farm. The horse had joined a wild herd of mares, resulting in Fireworks being born eleven months later. He always wished that he had never been caught in the round-up and sold. I never understood why he was not happy in a friendly place like Dewonberry stables, but I did admire his ability to tell stories and make decisions.

Jane walked towards me and talked quietly. I was glad the fighting was over. Jane calmed me until I stopped trembling.

"Okay, bring him over," George called in a hoarse voice.

The gate opened, Jane pulled the rope of my halter. I guessed the truth, my head shot up as fear galloped through my body. Before I could do any more, the gate was shut behind me. The halter pulled at my head and I was at the ramp. My whole body and soul were aching with fear and horror. I reared high, almost toppling backwards, as I swung round desperately and hopelessly trying to reach my mother. She screamed too, her front legs banging against the gate. I am sure she thought of trying to jump out, for she trotted back and forward, whinnying with all her might. I fought, but three strong men were too much for me and fairly soon succeeded in getting me next to the sweating skewbald, my friend Fireworks. George tied the rope and said a few gruff, but kind, words in my ear. A tear fell and landed on my chestnut hair. Before it had even trickled down to my nose, George had departed. I hardly noticed, for I stared at my mother. She shrieked for my return. I whinnied and whinnied. I pulled and tugged. The ramp banged shut, the engine started, the horse box moved. We called until only our own echoes returned. I wondered why there had to be pain in life. I felt alone.

Chapter Two

Hours later, the ramp was drawn down. I pricked up my ears and felt a tingle of excitement at the scene before me. Horses of all shapes and sizes were tied to rails, or loose in pens. Scruffy men were everywhere, shouting orders or inspecting horses. There were many different sorts of humans too, trying out horses or just looking around. Someone appeared and untied me. I held my head up high as I danced down the ramp, over the cobbles, into the pen. There was a good supply of hay waiting for me, but how could I eat in such excitement?

"Oh, Daddy, look, Isn't he gorgeous?"

The man agreed with his daughter, looking at me as he spoke.

"Now, come on, Lindy, we didn't come here to buy a yearling colt. He's no use to you so forget him."

"But Daddy, instead of getting a donkey to keep Blue company, we could buy him. Please Daddy, can't we? After two or three years I'd be able to ride him as well as Blue. I could take my friends riding with me. Daddy, please."

"Come on, Lindy," replied the man, walking past me. The girl hugged me and whispered, "I will have you."

She then followed her father to a nearby pen with a donkey in it.

"How about this, pet?" asked the father, looking into the eyes of an old grey donkey with long, floppy ears.

"He's too old, Dad, Blue might annoy him, or he might die."

"Well, this one looks full of life," replied the man, looking at the next donkey. It was about six years old, with a beautiful shiny brown coat and bright eyes. Lindy looked rather annoyed, probably because she could not think of a reason for not having that donkey. I thought of all the children in the stable who would have done anything to own such a pert, lively fellow as the donkey appeared to me. I should like to have made friends with him myself, but I heard Lindy mumble, "He'd be wasted with us. He's too good to just be a companion for a fretting horse."

"You might be right, Lindy. However, there is only one more donkey for us to look at. Why have you lost so much interest? You have pestered me for weeks. If it's the colt you're after, you know we can't afford him. You're darned lucky to be getting anything else. How many children would give their bottom teeth for the pony you've already got? How many, Lindy? Now enough of this nonsense. Do you want a donkey or not?"

"Don't be horrible, Daddy," said the girl, unfairly, "I did want one, ever so much, but now I've had a much better idea. Can't you see Dad, it would be far more sensible to have another horse?"

I could see that Lindy felt a bit unsure as to why it would be more sensible. She struggled on persuadingly.

"If I give you all my Christmas and Birthday money for the next five years, can we get the foal, please, Daddy?"

They were interrupted then by a friend of the man. I learnt that Lindy's father was called Mr. Dalford. Most of what they said I could not hear because Lindy had left the men to talk and had returned to my side. Whether they spoke about me or not I never knew, but when the man left, Mr. Dalford seemed to have a change of heart.

"I suppose we could sell him again in a couple of years and make a profit. You won't need two riding horses. Besides, you know we really can't afford the tack and shoeing a working horse needs. If you are prepared to find a good home for him in a couple of years time when he's due to be broken in, then I'll put in a bid for him."

"Great, Dad. Absolutely super. I love you."

Lindy flung her arms round the unemotional man, then round me. George appeared and told them all about me. The bidding began and in no time at all I was sold to the Dalfords.

It was arranged that Lindy would take me to my new home, herself. We both thoroughly enjoyed the six mile walk. Buds were pushing themselves out to make attractive blossoms all along the lane. Yellow daffodils coloured the grass verge, while in the fields Spring lambs frolicked gaily. A squirrel skipped over the lane and up a tree, then cheekily danced along a branch, stopping to watch me and Lindy. Lindy looked up at the little red, furry animal who cheekily returned the stare before running back along the branch and leaping onto the next tree, where he became hidden by leaves.

By the time we got to the farm it was dark. Mr. and Mrs. Dalford were waiting anxiously. Her father said it would be unwise to put me in the field with Blue immediately. I was put in a stall in the cowshed, where to my surprise, I fell asleep very soon.

The next day dawned fair. I was fed, then introduced to Blue. I had been looking forward to meeting the horse, whom I had been bought to keep company. Unfortunately the introduction did not go as well as planned.

We trotted towards each other intent on different purposes. I wanted to make friends with the charcoal grey gelding, but as I reached Blue, he swung round and lashed his hind legs out at me. What a shock I got, as his hoof, wearing a metal shoe, hit my side. I squealed and jumped angrily aside. "As if it was my choice to come here," I thought indignantly. I turned to tell the nasty, unfriendly horse that I really did not care for staying with him, but before I could utter a sound, Blue leapt at me and bit my neck viciously. What a beast he was. After all, I was still a youngster, I did not know how to fight. He came at me again, but I ran away. Lindy caught Blue and put him in the next field with the cows. She then tried to catch me, but I would not let her. I was rather annoyed, you see, and wanted to be on my own. She muttered something about school then ran off, collected a bag and disappeared out the gate.

I felt very sorry for myself and my side hurt. Many times I leaned over the fence and tried calling to Blue. He totally ignored me. I could see that he was plain jealous. Also, he did not like being in with cattle. Any time a cow approached him, he hastily moved away. I liked cows, but none of them were interested enough in me to have a chat.

I strolled over to the gate. To my surprise, as I touched it, the gate swung open. I wandered nervously into the deserted farm yard.

"Grunt, grunt, grunt. Snort."

"What on Earth can that be?" I wondered.

Following the snorts, I ventured behind the barn and found the pig sty. I had never seen a pig before and at that time wished never to see one again. I quivered in horror at the loud, fat creatures snorting in the mud. The biggest pig of all raised its snout and ran towards me. At the same time, a hen came squawking round the corner, chased by a colourful cock. This was too much for a nervous foal. I forgot the pain in my side and took off as quickly as possible. Leaving the farm behind, I galloped into the road. A blue mini car swerved to avoid me and landed with a thud in the ditch. My nerves in complete panic, I fled down the road. All I could hear were my hoof beats. With no thought of where I was heading, I moved faster and faster. Suddenly, another car, a loud horn, a screech of brakes and I was flying through the air. As I landed on the other side of a high hedge, for a fleeting moment I wondered what miracle had given me strength to clear such a height. Voices behind me were calling out.

"We've got to stop him."

"Yes, he'll hurt himself."

"Did you see that leap?"

"Come on, you go that way and I'll go left."

I was trapped in a garden. Nothing would persude me to jump such a high hedge again. I really had no time to think the first time. It had just appeared before me and was the only alternative to crashing into a car. Vegetables and flowers kept squashing under my hooves. A woman's face appeared at a window, she screamed.

CRASH. Oops, I had trodden on a glass frame, smashed it and cut my leg. This slowed me down. With a snort, I suddenly calmed down. At the same time the woman came out of the cottage and the two girls whom I assumed were from the car, appeared.

"Oh, you've caught him, Mrs. Watts. How on Earth did you calm him down? Whose horse is he?"

"How should I know? Look at the damage he's done. Are you sure he isn't one of your beasts?"

"Of course not. How dare you. As if we wouldn't own up," the younger blurted out.

"We'll take him home and tend to his leg. We'll find his owner and make sure they refund you," the older added.

They took me to their home, I soon found out from the other horses all about the girls.

Veronica was a rather naughty girl. She was seventeen and already had her own sports car, given to her by her very rich father. She always wore a lot of make up and permed her short, curly, brown hair, making the blonde streaks wave in all different directions. She would never ride in anything except the correct riding outfit. Denims were far too scruffy.

Her sister, Julia, was twelve. Both of them won many cups in horse-jumping competitions. They shared three horses between them. However, they quite often sold their horses and bought new ones. Money was no object. In fact, to these girls, the only thing that mattered was winning competitions, or leading the field on cross-countries. The third member of the Hartnell family was a boy named

Martin, who was car crazy and hated horses. Last, but best, was six year old Johnny. He was fun.

The family lived in a large country house surrounded by their own five fields, a jumping paddock and schooling ring. They even had their own groom who lived above the garage, beside their stables.

Chapter Three

I was to see Lindy only once while at the Hartnells. She spoke to me for a very long time, telling me in detail all about her home coming. It went something like this.

Her journey home from school had been enjoyable. She had felt happy, it was such a sunny day. She even told me the poem she had made up.

> "Sunbeams sailing on the trees,
> Birds are flying in the breeze,
> A butterfly did flutter by,
> While the sun keeps shining
> In the clear blue sky."

The open field gate was naturally a terrible shock. She gasped and ran at top speed to the house, yelling on her mother. Mrs. Dalford had not missed me and was as worried as her fretting daughter.

"I'll phone around and see if he is at any of the farms nearby. You go out and look for him Lindy, right away."

Lindy had shot out of the farm yard and luckily headed in the right direction. She went half a mile before she came to a house. It was the cottage belonging to Lily Watts, the woman whose garden I had landed in.

Lindy hammered at the door, probably scaring the poor woman out of her wits. The door opened.

"Have you ... seen a young ... pony ... he escaped?"

"What's that child? A pony? I certainly have. Come in, dear."

Lindy entered.

"Now take a deep breath and tell me what has happened, Lindy," the woman's soft voice commanded. Lindy had pulled herself together and explained to Mrs. Watts all about me. In turn, the woman told Lindy how I had jumped the hedge, then smashed a pane of glass. She showed Lindy the damage. Trampled flowers looked horrible.

"Is he alright, Mrs. Watts?"

"Yes. He's cut his leg on the glass frame, but he was quiet when he left here. Would you like a cup of tea, or a lemonade?"

Lindy had accepted the lemonade. She said she'd been in a real muddle then, scared to go home and tell her father and not nearly brave enough to go up to the Hartnells alone.

She soon returned home and was met at the gate by her father, wearing a face like thunder. He had already found out my whereabouts and of the crimes I had committed!

"Come inside, Lindy. I have to talk to you."

"Oh, can I just go and see Blue first?"

"LINDY."

"I'm coming."

Seated round the fireplace, Lindy's parents had begun to reason with her. Mr. Dalford began.

"Your mother has been in touch with the Hartnells. Mrs. Watts will have to be paid quite a sum of money for all the damage done."

"I'll pay, Daddy. Let me save up. Honestly I'll pay all of it, if it takes me years."

"That you may do, Lindy, but I'm afraid the vet's bills are going to be rather beyond your earning ability. Anzor has serious cuts on his legs which will have to be attended to. On top of all this, young Freddie down the road has asked us to pay for the repairs to his car. Apparently Anzor shot out in front of him and he had the choice of hitting him or landing in the ditch. He chose the latter course. We should have insured the pony."

By then, Lindy was speechless. Her father had continued for quite some time in his low monotonous voice. He had reminded her of the judge on a television programme she'd seen last week. I was the guilty person while she was the lawyer trying to defend me. I'd never seen television, but Lindy explained it very well.

Her father finished off, "...... and what's more, Blue obviously does not want company, therefore I see no reason for us to keep Anzor. He can not be put in with Blue again. No, Lindy, the odds are against him. He'll have to go."

Lindy had been silent then, tears trickling down her face. Her father started talking again.

"Don't worry dear. There's no need to be upset, everything is arranged. The Hartnell girls liked Anzor's style. He cleared Mrs. Watts hedge effortlessly and with a foot to spare. They believe he'll make a great jumper one day and are willing to take him off our hands. They will give us what we paid for him and of course the vet's bills will then be theirs. They've also agreed to settled Mrs. Watts' costs. What do you think, Lindy? I'll still get you a donkey if you want one."

"I hate the Hartnells." She ran from the room and found comfort with Blue.

That night, Lindy stole away and went to the Hartnells. She found me, alone in a loose-box. I was pleased to see her. She was very upset though, and had clung tightly to me while through her tears I heard the whole story I have just related. When she left me, after about an hour and a half, she kissed my forehead and said lots of nice things. It was all very sad.

I could hardly believe that this time two days before, I had been with my mother.

I stood alone in my loose-box. I could not sleep. The top half of the door was open, so I looked out. My eyes were heavy and tired. They stared unseeingly into the night. My heart and head were heavy too. I'll never forget that lonely, sleepless night. It was the first unhappy night I had ever had.

Chapter Four

For the next two years of my life, I was fairly content. Too young to be ridden, my days were passed dozing in daisy-covered fields, or watching and listening to the schooling of the other horses. The Hartnells were a bad-tempered lot, spending half of their time yelling at their horses and the other half arguing with each other.

Little Johnny was the exception. Unlike the others, he often talked to me, stroking my muzzle gently. It was Johnny's Shetland pony, Spooky, whom I grazed with most of the time. Spooky was a bundle of fun. Often we would gallop round the field together, or have a fun fight.

All things must pass however, and the time came for me to be broken in. Veronica and Julia walked over the field towards me. I felt suspicious of their determined stride and straight faces. Flattening my ears, I turned away and trotted to the far side of the field.

"Come here," demanded Veronica angrily.

She paused, then changed her tone.

"Come on, pony, stay there, that's a boy."

Actually, I felt rather too lazy to play games, thus decided I may as well let myself get caught and see what was in store for me.

They haltered me and we went to the stable-yard. As had happened before, I was bridled and saddled. I did not mind this procedure, but could never understand why anyone should want to dress me up, lead me around for a while, then remove the tack.

However, this time was to be different. To my surprise, almost before I realised, Julia was on my back. A surge of excitement swept through me. My hooves tingled at this strange extra weight. I side-stepped across the yard, dancing on the cobbles, to the sound of Julia's rather nervous voice. Her apprehension hit me and when she pulled my reins, the sensation of the bit in my mouth was too much. My instant reaction was to rear, and rear again, losing my passenger the second time.

Ow, my neck. Veronica cruelly whacked me on the neck with her crop. Julia swore and grabbed me from her sister. In doing so, she roughly pulled the bit, so that it rubbed my sensitive mouth. I jerked my head up, unsuccessfully trying to free myself.

By now I was frightened, but instead of calming me, the sisters tried again and again to mount me, until Julia once more sat upon my back. I did not mind Julia on my back, but the whites of my eyes must have shown my nervousness as I tried to free myself from Veronica. She let go of the reins at last. I stood quivering, unsure what to do when Julia squeezed me with her knees. The light pressure encouraged me to walk forward, although of course I had not yet been taught what the various commands meant.

"He's quietening down now," Julia said.

"Yes, but I think that'll do today. Perhaps we should have lunged him first. He's not going to be easy, is he?"

"I don't know. If he's going to make a habit of throwing me off, I'd rather sell him. After all, it's a brilliant jumper we're aiming at and if he's going to be a rearer, that's just no good."

"You're right, we'll see how he goes," Veronica concluded as we reached the field gate.

The next day I was lunged. I quite enjoyed this and stepped out proudly. Circles did get boring after a while though. When Julia decided to mount, she thrust her foot in the stirrup, while Veronica held my head. This callous approach annoyed me, so I side-stepped, much to their annoyance.

"That's your fault, Julia," cried out Veronica.

"My fault? What are you talking about? Don't be stupid."

"If you hadn't fallen off yesterday, he wouldn't be nearly so scared of you."

"My fault? Who hit him with the crop?" replied Julia curtly, as at last she swung her leg over the saddle.

I tossed my head, but I had nothing to worry about this time actually, for being kept on the lunge, I hardly felt the bit.

A few days of this exercise passed uneventfully, then Julia began to gather up the reins. She did so very gradually, until I really did not mind at all. In fact, as time went on, I learnt to enjoy being ridden, for at least I was taken out of the grounds into the colourful exciting forest.

There were days when I loathed the girls though. Perhaps a leaf would blow before me. I would leap aside in fun, only to have the whack of my rider's crop hit my side painfully. Or perhaps I would answer the whinny of a friendly pony in a roadside field, as it trotted towards the fence. Just a few seconds to blow down our noses and make friends with each other was all we wanted. Without fail, every time Julia pulled my head away and kicked me to go on. I wondered, did she ever stop long enough to listen to the sounds of Nature, to really hear the tunes each bird sings, or the magic whispering of the wind blowing through the trees.

I learned a lot in the next three months. I was ridden and groomed regularly. Luckily, strength and good health belonged to me. Unfortunately I had one bad fault which I could not overcome, this was nervousness. The girls with their stinging crops had upset my mind. I had jumped in pretend fright at surprise objects appearing before me, or at blowing paper bags. Each time the crop cutting my side made me jump a second time. In this way, I learnt to really fear anything out of the ordinary. I tried so hard to always be ready for a fright, because I did not want to jump aside and then be hit. The result was that I was always looking for danger and thus was very jittery and jumpy. I became difficult to catch and never quite happy about being groomed.

One day when Julia was brushing me, she dropped the dandy brush. Silly me, I leapt to the far side of the loose-box.

"You stupid horse, come back here," snarled the angry girl. "Boy, am I fed up with you."

She flung the brush down again, just to annoy me, then called on the groom to see to me.

Soon Julia and I were heading for my first public event, a "Pony Club" rally. The ride to the field took only half an hour. There were about thirty horses and even more people there.

"This is fun," I thought. I loved meeting other horse and held my head and tail up high, feeling a tingling excitement running through me. Obeying Julia, I trotted and cantered round the field. Definitely on my best behaviour. The afternoon passed smoothly with incident, until everyone stopped for a break.

Some people were having tea, others just relaxing. Julia shouted on a friend of hers and we trotted past some parked cars. CRASH! A woman dropped her tray of cups, plates and biscuits as she tripped over a halter. ZOOM! What a fright! I fled over the field, bumping into another horse on the way. That horse took off, leaving its rider sitting on the ground. The field had a high fence. Two steps and I was at it. Would I stop, or jump? Julia had no control, I swerved. She went straight on and hit the fence before she landed on the ground. My reins went flying, I caught my leg in them and tripped. I was not hurt and leapt up, but too late, I was caught by a burly man. I immediately took a dislike to this man, for no real reason, I was just sick of people.

More people gathered round, but before long a woman, who was apparently one of the Pony Club leaders; rode me quietly home. I felt stupid. I was tired now and didn't really care what happened to me. I knew I'd been silly to run off and I still remember the twanging of wires and the thud as Julia hit the ground.

"Was she hurt?" I thought to myself. "Perhaps she was dead."

I had heard that sometimes after an accident people and animals became dead.

"What was 'dead'"? I wondered.

I had never seen anything that way, so did not really know what it meant. The Hartnells had had a spaniel called Fluff. He had run out of the drive. I remember hearing a thud and yelp, then the dog had been carried in. That was the last time I had ever seen it. I had heard it had become this mysterious word "dead" though. I puzzled over this as I walked along, not caring how many leaves jumped at me.

The groom met us at the gate and took me inside. He was angry and spoke roughly but I didn't even bother listening. I was put out in the field without even a feed. Spooky was there so I went over to him and we talked quietly under the cherry tree.

"What is dead, Spooky?" I asked.

"Why? Don't you know? It's when you die, when you lie down and never get up again."

"I often lie down. If I never got up again would I be dead?"

"Oh, no, not like that. It's when you're old, or very ill, or have a bad accident. You go to sleep forever."

"But how do you know if you'll wake up or not? When will I die?"

"Oh, Anzor, it's not for you for a long time. I am old. One day, I know I'll feel tired, very tired, and I am sure I'll know which sleep will be my last one. Horses do know. It's just a feeling. I've seen it happen."

"What happens to you. Where do you go?"

"Ah, that I don't know. Don't think about it, Anzor, you're best not to think of these things. You'll never know all about it, for a dead horse can't tell tales. Forget it, Anzor, let's talk about something else."

"I still don't understand. Why? .... but ... oh, there are so many questions about Life. I am tired of those girls. The only life I enjoy here is in the meadow speaking to you. If you die, I'll be all alone and I'll die too."

"Anzor!" said Spooky, not liking this talk. "Please, talk about something else. What happened today?"

Chapter Five

I was left in that field for a week. Not one person came to speak to me. Spooky told me that Julia was in hospital. I never found out what happened to her, because on the seventh day I was put in a horse-box and driven far away to the outskirts of London, to a horse dealer.

I knew I would miss Spooky but was glad to be leaving that place of bad memories. With interest I walked down the ramp and looked around. I saw a cobbled yard, a huge dung heap and almost grass-bare fields. I smelt the stagnating pool of filth beside the dung heap. I smelt the cigarette spoke as it blew in my face. Soon I was to become used to this, for "Spike", as the dealer was called, was never without his cigarette. His fingers were yellow with nicotine. I felt apprehensive as I heard a couple of mournful whinnies. Nobody looked very happy. Spike was a skinny, fairly tall, dark man. He took me and put me in a stall, then left.

I turned to the pretty little bay mare beside me. She snapped at me visciously.

"Why did you do that?" I enquired.

"Habit, I suppose. Most horses here are bad-tempered. You soon will be too. My name's Petronella. Why are you here?"

"I don't know really. I suppose it's because I threw my rider off."

"That'll be right. Folk who can't sell their horses locally, send them to old Spike here. Plenty rich folk in London who want a horse, but hardly know one end from the other. That's the type he sells to. No decent folk would buy from him. If there are any decent people left."

I did not really believe Petronella for I had never had a very bad home and at least all my owners had cared for me sufficiently.

Petronella went on, "I'm here because I bite, and I have no intention of stopping. If they can't treat me properly, then I won't behave for them. Why should I be pushed around?"

"Have you been here long, Petronella?"

"Too long. He hires us out you know, until he sells us. We get all sorts here. They pull at your head, kick you, he doesn't care. As long as he gets his money. Spends it all on drink too. You'll see. Just you wait and see."

I had never been in a stall before. Used to a free head in a loose-box, I felt most uncomfortable having a weight tied to the end of the rope attached to my too big and cracked, hard, head collar. I liked to have my head up, but couldn't be bothered supporting the weight. Not even any hay to nibble at, I became bored.

Spike soon relieved my boredom when he came to look me over. He prodded me and lifted my feet, then slung a saddle on, pulling my girth far too tight. My head was thrust into a bridle. I held my head high until Spike cracked me on the neck, pulling it down, to force the bit between my teeth. Never a word to me, he hauled me out of the stable, leapt on and gave me a crack of his whip.

"I'll show you who's boss," he laughed, and dug his heels into my trembling sides. Into the open field, we cantered round and round. Spike pulled me up so suddenly that I squealed. My mouth hurt terribly. He put me through all my paces. I was exhausted, I had never been ridden like this before. All sudden starts or stops, tight pulls at the reins and frequent use of the crop. I was a willing horse and would canter with a gentle urging from the legs. Spike was ruining me.

At last, sweat dripping off both of us, the trial ended. Saddle off, bridle off, and alone in the field with no grass. I never slept a wink.

Next day I was put in with the other horses, a shabby lot.

"Do I look like them?" I wondered. "I hope not."

Big scrawny creatures, balding ponies, lame ponies, coughing ponies. There were a few fairly decent types though. No-one bothered with me so I trotted up to a huge skewbald.

"Hello, can I talk to you?"

"If you want to."

We both stood there. One sided conversations didn't appeal to me, I hung my head and sadly walked away. Closing my eyes, I remembered my mother. Where was she now? Where would I go next? If horses cried, I would have been weeping.

Sensing my loneliness, Petronella approached me. On her way over, another horse crossed her path. She swung round and kicked him, then without looking back walked on. I could not understand such behaviour.

"Petronella, why did you kick him? He didn't mean to get in your way."

"Why shouldn't I kick him. Lazy old brute needed waking up. No point in dreaming over here, Anzor. Come and I'll make some of them talk to you."

Anzor followed meekly. He met Fred, a big, dapple, ex-racehorse. He'd been a winner but as soon as he stopped making money, had been sold. He'd been tried out yesterday and thought he was leaving the next day for a city riding stable. He'd heard them say, "He should be okay in the city. A racehorse's used to crowds."

Next, I met Beauty, a brown, shaggy Shetland pony. She looked fine.

"Where have you come from?" I asked.

"I had a lovely home. I was owned by a beautiful little girl called Jacqueline. I lived there in a field behind their cottage all my life. Then, one rainy day they got killed in a car crash. They'd no close relations and everything was sold. I know there are good people in the world. I'm sure I'll go to a good home. I hope so. We, that is Jacqueline and her parents, used to go for picnics in the summer and often I'd be taken into their garden and tethered to a post. Jacqueline's friends would come and play. I was always the centre of attention. It was super."

The next horse I met was very poorly. He was about 14 h.h., dark brown with big sad eyes and a matted tail. He said he had had so many names that he was sick of them. Who wanted a name anyway? He coughed and wheezed, his ribs heaving with the effort each time. He had no pleasure in life, didn't even enjoy eating. He had been a barrow pony in London as his last "job". The man had bought a stand in a market and given up selling round the streets.

"Thank goodness," the pony said. "He didn't hardly feed me or care for me. He didn't even give me a name."

Our peace, if you could call it that, was interrupted by a family arriving in a crowded car. Out jumped three boys of about eight, nine and ten, followed by a huge man and a skinny, bored looking woman.

Spike greeted them and said all would be ready in a minute. The huge untalkative skewbald, Beauty, myself and two others were all caught and quickly saddled and bridled. The family mounted, the woman on me, and off we went, walking slowly.

"Ooooh, isn't this fun," giggled my rider.

Her husband laughed and dug his heels into the skewbald.

"Come on, let's trot."

We trotted, riders bumping up and down, reins being pulled, stirrups lost, cars hooting us, for we spread across the road. This continued for some time. We turned up a quiet side road and the littlest boy yelled,

"Watch me Mummy," dug his heels in, then careered along the road at a fast canter. Beauty was obeying him. Did she not realise how bad it was to canter on tarmac?

The ride ended, all in one piece, an hour later. Fred had gone to his new home. Someone else, a man of about forty, was looking for a horse. The skewbald was the only horse big enough for him, so he got on and away they went for a trail ride. Meantime I was hired out to another young woman whose boyfriend was on the horse with no name. We set off walking. I don't think either had ever been on a horse before. "No name" kept coughing and the boy kept pulling his head up. Why did he not realise that it was difficult to cough properly with your head up. "No name" was urged into a trot by the boy. The girl on me just sat, but I decided I'd better trot after them. She clung on to my mane and yelled at the boy to stop. "No name" stopped willingly. I did likewise, but the poorly horse would not walk on. He just stood and coughed. Half an hour later, we were still standing there.

"No name" had been pulled, pushed, slapped, gently urged and yelled at. He would not budge. An hour later, the boy and girl were sitting happily chatting at the side of the road, holding onto our reins. I suppose they knew when they didn't return, someone would come looking for them. They had made attempts to move the horse, every ten minutes or so, with no luck.

Spike did arrive. He drove up and asked them what the heck they were doing, their time was up half an hour ago. After explanations, he grunted and mounted the old tired horse.

Whack! lashed the whip on his side, whack, whack, whack, again. I felt pain inside my head at the very sight.

"No name" just stood shaking. He never uttered a sound. More whacks until I saw blood on the horse's neck. Suddenly, he reared up, squealed a moan like I have never heard and fell to the ground, dead. Now I knew what Spooky had talked about. Here, my inquisitive mind was witness to death. "No name" had surely known his time was up. I heard later he'd had a bad heart. He lay there with unseeing eyes.

The girl screamed and buried her head into the boy who thrust her aside. This meek character's mind had opened and he caught Spike by the arm, twisted him round and punched and punched him till blood spurted out of his nose.

A passing car had called the police. I was taken to the stable while all the people were taken away somewhere.

In the field, I told the sad tale, ending with, "I don't know where they took the horse with no name."

To cut a long story short, Spike got off light. No one could prove that he knew the horse was ill because the couple knew nothing about horses. Apparently the body had been done away with before the police could check the truth of the vicious whipping. The boy was charged with assault but got off, thank goodness, due to the judge believing he was upset at the horse's death. "Is that human justice?" we thought. It is okay for a man to hit a horse, but not to do so to another man.

I was at the stable for five weeks. In that time, many horses came and went. My coat became dull and I lost a lot of weight. I also lost my beliefs in many things, but I never lost hope.

"Without hope of something better to come, how could we continue?" I said to the others. I had become a leader in the stable, cheering up the depressed horses by telling them that as soon as they accepted their present state as "life", then they might as well give up.

"We must fight back," I said. "Remain strong and active. The better we look, the better homes we may go to. Don't give up. We will make better lives for ourselves."

I am sure I stirred the hearts and souls of the horses. Their lost dreams of happy homes returned. Their eyes began to sparkle, although they could not make their coats shine. Then one day Beauty was sold to a little girl. She said she was almost as pretty and kind as Jacqueline.

"She doesn't know about horses," she said, "but I'll teach her."

Off she went, full of hope.

Chapter Six

At last my turn came. The prospective buyer was a girl called Alison, who arrived with her father and mother.

"How about this one, Mr. Smith?" suggested Spike, "nice quiet horse, lovely teeth, look." He hauled my mouth open.

"He's a lovely colour," said Mrs. Smith.

"He's a fine size," said Alison.

"How much?" asked Mr. Smith.

They argued over the price, then Mrs. Smith suggested, "Let's leave them to it, dear, and we'll try the horse."

She helped the girl on.

"Ooh, Mummy, don't let go of me."

She had never been on a horse before. They walked round.

"Ooh, this is a funny feeling. Please let's get him, Mummy, please. I'm going to call him Tree."

"Tree? Whatever for? That's a strange name. Can't you think of something better?"

"How about 'Chestnut' because that's his colour?"

"I can't see you going out and calling 'Chestnut' or 'Tree'. How about 'Tommy' or 'Foxy'?"

"No, I've decided now I'm going to call him "Chestnut Tree', he can be 'Nutty' for short."

Thus I became Nutty. I always thought of myself as Anzor though.

That same day, without even being able to say goodbye to my friends, I was taken for an hours drive, to my new home. There were houses all around. The field was a small area of rough ground with quite a lot of trash in it. Peoples back gardens led onto the field on three sides. The other side led onto a road. There was no stable nor any trees to shelter under.

"This is what my hopes have led me to," I thought sadly. However, here at least I was to be loved.

Alison doted on me. She spent lot of her time just talking to me and stroking my face. Often she would plait my mane just for fun. Yet she was scared to ride on the road. For weeks I was in that field. Alison's father would lead her around when she rode me. She loved that, but would not go on her own.

There was not much in the way of good grass and very often I felt extremely hungry. The Smiths' ignorance proved very painful for me. Instead of having regular supply, a bucket of water was left out each morning. If I finished it, no-one thought of a refill. Sometimes at night, local boys would jump on my back. I never bit any of them, as I know they didn't mean any harm.

Winter came, as did the snow. I was used to being inside on cold winter nights. Having to brave the elements was a new and unwelcome experience.

One day as Alison fondled me, she said, "Oh, Nutty, you're getting so thin, can't you dig through the snow for grass? You are lazy. What do you think wild ponies do?"

I was absolutely horrified. Was I really never going to be fed? I would have to do something about this.

That night, I planned to get out of the field and find food. My stomach ached and rumbled with hunger.

The wall between the road and the field was not too high. Why had I not thought of this before? As soon as the streets became quiet and lights went out, I trotted up and down alongside the wall. Perhaps it was quite high after all I decided and looked over. At least no ditch on the other side. I trotted back from the wall then cantered towards it. "Stop, I can't do it," I thought. But on my second attempt I did, clearing it easily. As this was the first time I had ever been out of the field, I had no idea where to go. I decided it was great to be trotting free, with no rider and no fence around me. My joy was short-lived.

"Hoy, come back here," a man shouted.

As if I would obey! I cantered on, hooves clattering in the dark. Lights went on or curtains drew back, but I was going to be free forever, I had quite decided.

At last, grass, lush grass, sprouting above the thin layer of snow. Turning into the food-filled garden, I mingled amongst the trees and ate to my heart's content, not having felt so happy for months. I ate and slept well until dawn, when the city sounds awoke me. Birds, buses, cars, cats, people and dogs. I stayed amongst the trees until a man in a very blue uniform carrying a big brown bag over his shoulder turned into the drive. He looked at me, came closer, then went up to the front door and rang the bell.

"Excuse me, did you know there's a horse loose in your garden?" he said as he handed over the letters.

"Oh, no. HENRY!" the upset lady called.

I decided it was time to go and trotted onto the drive and then the pavement. Pedestrians jumped out of my way or tried to catch my head. It was horrible. I knew my freedom would soon end, there was no way out of this jungle of buildings, cars and people. After some time, I noticed a van draw up in front of me. It had R.S.P.C.A. on the side. The man climbed out, he looked friendly and carried pony nuts and a head collar. I felt a surge of relief on seeing a horsy-type person, and did not fight him. His friend drove off while he led me to a fairly nearby small stable, that I didn't even know existed. There was an empty loose-box, into which I was put and actually given a feed, a luscious bran mash. It tasted absolutely divine.

Meanwhile, Alison must have discovered I was missing. I wondered what she was thinking. My break had certainly been worthwhile, whatever happened.

The man came back.

"Well, you're a skinny beast. I wonder where you come from? I'm sure we'll find out soon enough," he said patting me hard on the neck. At that moment a Police car arrived with Mr. Smith.

"That's him," he said. "That's Alison's Nutty."

"This horse is half-starved. What do you feed him on?"

"Grass of course, he's not stabled. He lives out, in a field."

The man took Mr. Smith aside and they had a long chat. Eventually, I was taken back to the field and fed on hay and oats. That evening when Alison rode me, the oats worked inside and I felt very fresh. I kept trying to trot until she got scared and dismounted. I liked Alison, but was so bored with this one field existence. This was not living. I planned to misbehave so that I would be sold. I knew it was bad to think like that, yet I could not overcome the urge. For a couple of weeks, I built my strength up. I ate lots of oats and hay. If Alison would not exercise me, I'd exercise myself. I cantered up and down, round and round that field. I practiced extended trots and I leapt over pretend jumps. Always I had an audience, passers-by and people from the neighbouring houses stood and watched the performance. I lapped this up, as I did the carrots and sugar they brought me. I was in the prime of my life. I would not grow old and stale letting life pass by. My muscles built up now and I heard some knowledgeable people state that they could see the Arab in me. Of course, my father was a champion. What was I doing here?

At last I became so vain that Alison was scared of me. Of course I would never have hurt her, I just liked playing games. It was fun not to let her catch me, to trot round her in circles, the crowd laughed. Looking back, I feel embarrassed for poor Alison. I was so full of myself and so determined to leave the Smiths that I could not see how I was hurting her. At night, in the dark, I was quiet. Alison and I were friends then. One night she told me that she loved me more than anything else in the world but that she knew I needed a more active life. How understanding of her. She was the first human I loved.

The next day a "Horse for Sale" sign went up on my gate. My vanity had gone as quickly as it came. I now felt nervous. Where would I go next? I still exercised myself, but for my own pleasure, not to show off.

Two days after the notice went up, a woman and her husband, driving a Land Rover, passed by slowly, watching me. They stopped as I continued trotting and cantering up and down. The next time I looked they had gone. I did not know it then, but they had gone up the road to the Smiths' little house. Soon the whole lot, the Smiths and the couple, arrived in the field. I trotted keenly over to them. The woman rode me round the field. It was so long since I'd been ridden by a proper rider that I did not please her as well as I should have. The deal was made, however and in less than a week I had said goodbye to Alison and was on my way into the unknown, again.

Chapter Seven

A long ride in a good, airy horsebox, took us to a lovely part called the New Forest. I actually saw some free ponies roaming on a village green. Wasn't this where my mother was from? We had talked so much yet I don't know if she was born wild or in a stable. What a pity I hadn't thought to ask.

It was a sunny day. Oh, what joy to leave the city far behind. What joy to see trees again and lots of them. I felt my whole spirit fill with power.

We turned in a gateway. Out the front of the horsebox, I saw fields surrounded by white wooden fencing. Horses grazed peacefully. We came to a halt. I was led onto a concrete yard with two rows of loose-boxes. I was lucky. My hope, I was sure, had paid off at last. Ponies whinnied a welcome, I whinnied in return. In the loose-box, there was straw on the floor, a hay net hung in one corner and there was a funny looking metal saucer in another. I pushed my nose into the saucer to see what I could find. Oh! I jumped.

When I pushed the metal tongue, it filled up with water. Surely this was heaven. I leant over the half door. A dapple-grey gelding next door spoke to me.

"Hello, I'm Misty, Sea Mist, actually. I do believe you're new here."

"How observant," I thought. I said, "Yes, I've just come from London. What kind of work do we do here? It's a lovely place."

We're a riding stable. In Summer there are gymkhanas and lots of day rides. It's all go. They need to look after us well, because we work really hard. The hours are very long."

"I'm not sure what they'll call me, but my name's Anzor. I've stayed in a few places but I'm sure this is going to be the best, since the place I was born, of course."

I was left to rest for that day. The next day I was turned out into the paddock by Jill, the groom. She had fair hair with long pigtails, was quite small, a little overweight and had lots of energy. After school and at weekends, two other girls and a boy helped. They were ten year old Kevin who worked in return for the odd ride, and Susan and Diane, who worked very hard but still paid for their rides. You see, they didn't have to come, they came because they enjoyed it. They all approved of the Mathieson's new horse, me. That Saturday afternoon Mrs. Mathieson took me out for a ride. The stable was swarming with people and absolutely all of the horses were out being ridden. We went on our own. I'll never forget that ride.

We left by a narrow track, with trees on both sides. Then we turned off and passed a field where the first Spring lambs were frolicking gaily. There were lots of birds flying and singing. I heard Mrs. Mathieson join in the merriment. She was enjoying herself. We crossed a bridge over a fresh, wide stream, then she turned back, crossed the bridge again and urged me to jump over the stream. I did, then I felt confident enough to ask her to do something for me. I pulled my head to the side until she loosened the reins to see where I wanted to go. I walked back to the stream and had a drink. It was cool, fresh and delicious. We continued on into the wood. A little roe deer darted in front of me. I was so relaxed I hardly even jumped. Through the woods, across some open land and into more quaint paths. We had a few gentle canters but nothing too fast. Everything was just right.

Back at the stable, Diane took care of me while Mrs. Mathieson went off to see some customers. I was turned out with the only horse not working a pure white, dainty Arab horse. She called me over.

"Hello, Shanti."

"How do you do, but Shanti isn't my name. It's Anzor."

"Well actually, only this morning I heard Mrs. Mathieson telling her husband she'd decided to call you Shanti. She said it meant "Peace" in the Indian language and that after your noisy home of before, she hoped you'd find it more peaceful here."

"Oh! Yes, I quite like Shanti. I prefer Anzor though."

The mare had a very haughty tone in her voice, I soon found out why.

"Did you enjoy your exercise?"

"Oh, yes, Mrs. Mathieson's super."

"She won't be riding you again. She takes out every new horse once. You see I am her special horse. My name is Sharine. No-one else rides me. Only Mrs. Mathieson."

I was angry. Why should this horse try to spoil my day. I replied that I was sure there were many others as nice as her and walked off. I didn't mean what I said, but I was hurt and couldn't think of a good reply. Later I thought of plenty things I could have said, but that wasn't much use.

That night I had a dream. I dreamt I was a flying horse. I had huge pink wings and wore a pink satin cloak over my chestnut body. The chestnut shone as brightly as a flame. I flew up to a bright star. The flight took a long time. On the way I had to jump aside from shooting stars. Then a black horse ridden by Spike reared up in front of me. Just as he was about to land on me, the horse turned into a butterfly and Spike to a little insect which with a quick lash of its tongue, the butterfly ate. On the star, I met my mother. I flew down to her, she reared up to greet me, then I woke up. What a strange dream. I don't remember any dreams normally, so I could not sleep any more that night for thinking about it. Imagine floating up into the sky. It had seemed so real.

The next day, my work really began. I will tell you everything I did that Sunday. I was awake early, due to the dream mentioned. I nibbled at some hay and had a drink before my stable was mucked out. Susan mucked out the box. She sang as she did so. When she wasn't singing, she had a very coarse voice and in fact loved ordering people around although she was just a child herself. I didn't ever take to her too much.

After being mucked out, I was given a small feed. Exactly at 9 a.m. (I heard the church bell in the nearby village) Kevin took me out of the stable. He'd chosen to have his free ride on me. He was nice and light, quite a good rider, but used his heels far too much. We had a hack with six other horses. Kevin kept holding me back then making me canter to catch up with the rest. It was fun.

From ten to eleven, a small man rode me. We went around the same track. He was quite a good rider too, but held my reins too tightly. Eleven o'clock, gosh, I wasn't as fit as I'd imagined, I was tired already. For the next hour, a little girl rode me. She was having a lesson. She had ridden before a fair bit. This was not as much fun as a hack, going round in circles never is.

Thank goodness for lunch hours. I was put in my box for two hours to rest and nibble my hay. A girl of about ten or eleven with huge blue eyes and dark hair came and hung over the loose box door. I ignored her due to my tiredness. She didn't actually say anything for me to ignore, but I mean I continued eating the hay.

"Hello, Ann. Do you like Shanti?" Jill asked.

"He's just the horse I've always dreamt of having, Jill. Just the right height and he's even got the blaze and four white socks that my dream chestnut pony had. He's adorable."

How nice. There's one thing about me, I love to hear myself spoken well of. I decided I would approach her after all, once Jill had gone. I ambled across the loose box casually.

"Oh, Shanti, you are so very beautiful," she whispered.

I felt my cheek tingle as she stroked it, blowing warm air down her nose onto mine, as one horse does to another to make friends. I blew warm air on her and after this ceremony, we became very good friends. She never talked too much, but her presence was very comforting. I felt very sorry at two o'clock that day when I was led out for another hack, for I did not know that I would see the girl again.

Another girl rode me for a two hour hack from two to four. I must say it was great. We went quite far into the forest and even saw some wild ponies. That was the last ride of the day. Ann was still there when I got back. She led me to my box, untacked and groomed me. That Sunday was quite typical of a Sunday. Saturdays were even busier. During the week we normally only had to do two or three hours of work a day which wasn't bad at all.

Then Easter came. Boy, did I work like I'd never worked before. Two weeks of school holidays and I was ridden about five hours each day. All the other horses worked equally hard, except of course for Mrs. Mathieson's precious Sharine.

The day treks were the best fun. Ann went on one, one day. She always rode me if she could. Her parents let her have one ride a week. On this ride, there were seven other horses. One was a new horse, a Highland called Dougal. Ann's friend Jenny rode Dougal. They rode abreast each other which gave me plenty time to get to know him.

Dougal was a strong, beautiful pony, about 14 h.h. He had been born in a Highland Pony Stud Farm in Scotland. His first year, as with me, was spent with his mother. He'd been bought by a private stable who had kept him until he was ready for breaking in. They broke him in and sold him at a profit to a Trekking Centre. He'd spent five pleasant years there. In the summer they took people of all shapes and sizes on treks up and down the Scottish Highlands. The pace was slow, the scenery beautiful and the air fresh. He told me about all the pheasant and grouse. He told me about the herds of red deer, led by powerful stags with huge antlers, who would stop and watch the trekkers with interest. I could not really imagine the mountains, bare of trees, covered in purple heather, going on forever as far as the eye could see. It sounded lovely.

They had had long rests by mountain streams and cooled off on the occasional very hot days by wading through a river. In winter there was no work. For his first three cold seasons he was turned out to graze with the twenty other ponies. The next two winters, he was given a home at a hill farm, where he was ridden now and then, keeping him fit for the next trekking season.

A man from the hill farm became a gamekeeper and bought Dougal. Thus for two years he had been a gamekeeper's pony. He'd had to carry down from the hills a couple of hinds at a time in the hind-shooting season or at other times, perhaps an old stag. He said it used to sicken him as he hated dead things, but apparently some deer had to be killed otherwise there'd be too many, thus not enough food and some would starve. Despite that, he'd enjoyed the work, although it involved going out in all weather. He loved the mountains dearly. The gamekeeper changed his job and the new one had his own pony. Dougal was sold to a family in the North of England who only kept him a week as just after buying him they found what they called "the horse they'd always been looking for." His next home was further South again. It was a dealers' stable, as the family before had wanted rid of him quickly to leave room for their new horse.

Dougal had not been at the dealers for long when he was bought by a man looking for a strong horse to pull a trap. Dougal never took to this kind of work. The man gave up and decided a car was less bother, thus Dougal reached his fourth home in six weeks, which was the Mathiesons' stable. The man with the trap was a good friend of Mr. Mathieson and he'd sent the horse down to him as a present, for he was a kind hearted man who had actually been fond of Dougal. He'd told Dougal he would give him away rather than sell him to what may be a bad home. He did just that.

Chapter Eight

Summer was approaching. Life was still busy, but good. Preparations were being made for an oncoming Gymkhana. Ann had hired me for that day. For the last few weeks, on her hourly ride, we had practised either jumping, going round poles or she jumping on and off of me. It was fun. Nobody had ever jumped me much before. The Hartnells had just started training me before I left them. Since then, apart from jumping out of my field by Alison's home, I don't think I had ever jumped at all. This new experience was exciting. Ann sometimes jerked my mouth, but I knew she didn't mean to. Jill noticed this and showed her how to run her hands down my neck a bit. That helped a lot. I enjoyed jumping little jumps but wasn't took keen on the big one. I didn't mean to be awkward when I refused, I just didn't have enough confidence. Sometimes I'd tackle them and manage fine, but I hated knocking them down. You know how I hate it when things fall down, whether they are dandy-brushes, buckets, cups and saucers or jumps!

The big day approached. Since the Pony Club Rally with Julia, I hadn't been to any public events. I was ever so nervous and hoped I wouldn't make a fool of myself this time.

The gymkhana was only four miles away so we'd ridden quietly over. What a big crowd. All the local people, plus lots of holiday makers thronged amidst the horses. Ann had groomed and groomed me. I knew if the sun came out, my coat would look shiny, but it was a very grey day, threatening rain.

A girl on a blue roan pulled up alongside us.

"Ann, that pony you're on, he's Anzor."

"What? The Anzor you told me about?"

"Yes, I know it is."

She dismounted and stroked my neck.

"Oh, Anzor, I'm so glad to see you happy," and she burst into tears of relief.

Ann dismounted and the two of them walked together. I learnt that Lindy Dalford who had bought me at the horse auction had lived a hundred miles away. Her parents had gone to the Persian Gulf for two years, leaving her with her Aunt Joan, whom they were going to live with when they came home. Aunt Joan's home was a farm not far from the gymkhana field. She and Ann were at the same school. I reminded Blue who I was and he apologised for his behaviour on our last meeting a few years before. We stopped talking and listened to the girls. Lindy was a year older than Ann. They enjoyed each others company obviously, but it seemed as if this was their first meeting as friends rather than as acquaintances.

"Are you sure it's Anzor?"

"Yes, positive, because just under his left ear he has a tiny patch of white hair, almost in the shape of a horse shoe. Even without that I'd be sure it was him. I used to sometimes see him at the Hartnells, though he didn't see me as I never dared go up their drive, except for once, the first night he was taken there. He threw his rider off at a Rally and was sold to a dealer. It broke my heart because there was absolutely nothing I could do about it. I never even managed to find out which dealer it was. He was only about four then. How long ago was that? Let me think, oh, two years at least. You say he's been at Mathiesons six months, I wonder where he was in between. He seems to have been well looked after."

I wished so much that I could tell them my story and the story of the horse with no name. I wondered, "Do good people realise how many cruel and ignorant people there are?"

The loudspeaker took me back to reality. Lindy and Ann parted after arranging to meet for tea the next day. The first event I was entered in was jumping. The meeting had awoken new interest in me. I not only wanted to prove to myself and Ann that I could jump, but also to Lindy. I didn't want to let anybody down, not anyone who believed in me.

I thought of the deer I'd seen flying over fences or fallen trees. I imagined I was wearing the pink wings of my dream. To get to the Paradise Star, instead of missing shooting stars, I had to avoid knocking down jumps. Having conditioned my mind into believing I was half deer and half flying horse, I entered the ring, closed my ears to the noise and made a clear round. Ann was as delighted as myself. She hugged me so hard it hurt. I relaxed now that

I thought that was over and went into a daydream of myself as a deer. I was rudely awoken by the words spoken by Jill to Ann.

"I wonder how he'll do in the jump off. You're the fifth clear round. There's only one more to jump."

"Oh, no," I thought. "I can't go through all that again. It's a terrible mental strain."

Then I saw Sharine strut by, with a red rosette on her bridle. She had won her Showing Class.

"I don't need to dream," I told myself. "I'll jump those jumps. I'll jump them as "Anzor," as my mother would want me to, and I won't knock any down." I told and persuaded myself this six times until it was our turn again. I remembered how I'd enjoyed the crowds watch me when I was in Alison's field. Why should I not have as much confidence here. I trotted into the ring and felt like bolting out. Looking round at all the people, I felt so scared, I trembled, I shut my ears to the noise, summoned up all my courage and we were off. I don't remember a thing. It was as if it was another horse jumping, but we did it. We had the only second clear round and I won a red rosette. Ann was delighted as we got a small silver trophy too. We had a picnic lunch with some others from the stable. Frisky, a cream coloured Welsh Mountain pony, was tied next to me. She was as gay as they come, a real bundle of energy. Today was no different. Kevin was riding her in the afternoon.

It began to rain about three o'clock. Frisky and Kevin had won the Musical Chairs and the pole bending race. They had also come second in the obstacle race. I hadn't been anywhere near winning anything else. The last event I was entered in was Musical Chairs Group 2. Here I helped Ann by also looking for the nearest empty stool. We came in third. After the jumping, an American man had asked if I was for sale. Ann, pretending to be my owner had said, "No, definitely not." Now, he approached again.

"Tell Mrs. Mathieson I'll be along on Thursday to see that horse."

Before Ann could say a thing, he walked off.

"He must have read the catalogue listing all the horses and owners" I heard Ann mumble to herself. "I won't tell Mrs. Mathieson."

Chapter Nine

I had forgotten all about the American, until he arrived. Ann was grooming me when she heard the unmistakable accent in the yard. She nipped out of my box and I heard her go on with Frisky and Kevin who were next door. Their whispers stopped as Mrs. Mathieson and the man approached.

"This is the beauty I'm talking about, Madam. I sure as heck would like to buy this here horse for my little girl."

"Well, I hadn't really thought of selling Shanti, Mr. Harper, he's a good horse, a lot of use to me and not very easy to replace."

"I'll give you what he's worth and half again, lady. It'll be worth it to see the joy on my baby's face when I tell her this little horse here's my present for her. Just you name your price and I'll see what I can offer."

"Well, Mr. Harper, let's go in for a coffee and talk this over. I'm not quite sure whether to consider your offer." They walked inside.

"She'll sell," stated Kevin.

"She'd better not," squealed Ann.

"I hope not," I thought.

"She's only trying to up the price, Ann. Mrs. Mathieson is a business woman. She needs money to keep going. That's why she keeps horses. There's just no way she won't sell. She'll make a good profit. After all, what's Shanti, or Anzor as you now call him, to her? She has her own special horse. She can't love all her horses."

Ann bit her lip. She was determined not to cry.

Kevin went on. "Don't start getting all het up, Ann. I know it's tough. The same thing happened to me with Jet. True, I still miss him, but I'm just as fond of Frisky now, as I was of him. Anzor'll get a good home. There'll be other horses."

Footsteps. Kevin and Ann stopped talking.

"Well, little horse. You belong to me now. You've got a long journey. You're going all the way to the U.S.A. You'd better be good, horse, 'cause if my little girl doesn't like you, I'm going to be one heck of an angry daddy. See you on Saturday."

He strode off.

"I can't make him out, Kevin. What do you think?"

"I dunno. He acts real big and tough, yet he seems awful soft. You're right Ann, I can't make him out, either. He sure dotes on his little girl, though. I bet she's a spoiled brat."

"Why should she be? I would love it if my dad bought me Anzor. I wouldn't feel spoiled, just lucky."

"Yes, but to buy a horse here when he could get one in the States. Still, I suppose if you've got lots of money it wouldn't make much difference. Perhaps they cost a lot more to buy over there."

"I'm going to see Anzor." Ann left Kevin and came back to my box.

"Anzor, oh Anzor, I wonder if you want to go. Will you like it there? What can I do, Anzor? I've been saving money for a pony but I don't have nearly enough yet. I so hoped that one day you'd be mine."

Her floods of tears really soaked my neck. I decided I didn't fancy going to America. It may be good, it may not, but I liked it here. I couldn't see a way out though, no way at all.

Ann cried nearly all of the rest of Thursday and Friday. Kevin tried hard to comfort her. He hadn't dared tell what he knew about the American from his father, who'd done business with the man. He was a businessman who came over every year. Earlier, while grooming me, Kevin had told me all about the man. He had no idea that I understood, so I assume he was really talking to himself. Harper was very rich and thought money could buy anything. Apparently the bringing back a present of a pony was almost a tradition. He had four daughters. His wife was now dead. Each year a pony was taken back as a present. The pony was kept until the girls went back to their boarding school in Switzerland. It was then sold cheaply to the local stable on the condition that the girls could have it back, if they wanted it, the following summer. By the next summer the new horse had been brought over so there was no guarantee that, after ten months without the pony, they'd want it at all. The local riding stables' five best horses had been originally bought by Mr. Harper. The man thought it was all a great laugh. It gave him the reputation of having a good eye for a horse, or so he thought. The Riding Stable liked to advertise "British horses", because they do have a good reputation.

Perhaps Harper just wanted to remain friends with the stable-owner by doing him favours.

Friday night was dark and wet. I was dozing in the field when the adventure began.

"Sash, quietly, here Anzor, come on boy. Here boy."

Kevin appeared, haltered me and led me to the gate. Some of the other horses stirred. Kevin stopped until there was silence again. A car's headlights shone up the drive. Kevin fell alongside the water trough and muttered something. A car door banged. Shouts of "Goodnight." Lights on in the house. First the downstairs light went on, then the staircase. Poth lights went off. Bathroom light on, bedroom light on. The former off, the latter off, darkness.

"Phew, that was close," signed Kevin. "Come on."

I had no idea where we were going, but I trusted Kevin. We must have walked for two hours. Thank goodness we had moonlight. At last we stopped. Kevin took the halter off and whispered.

"Goodbye for now, Anzor, keep safe."

He walked away, I followed him.

"No, Anzor, no. Go away, for your own sake. Please."

He ran away and left me standing in the dark. Puzzled I most certainly was. I didn't feel safe at all, out there in those dark woods alone.

"Screeeeech."

I jumped in horror. Only some kind of bird I decided. Then I noticed two eyes looking at me, glistening in the moonlight. I froze in fear. What a coward I am sometimes. The shadow and eyes disappeared. Probably a deer, I thought.

"What am I complaining about?" I asked myself. "Here I am free, why don't I enjoy it? I'm sure it won't last forever".

I'm not normally a slow thinker, but it just dawned on me then what Kevin was doing. I had been so excited at going out in the night that I had not realised that of course this was to save me from being shipped to the States. Dear Kevin, he's done this for Ann, I'm sure. In that case I'd better hide properly. I've often been here on treks. I'd better get further into the woods and keep well out of the way for a few days. I worked my way carefully through the woods, happy to know I had friends. Instead of being scared, I appreciated the peace of night. I looked at the stars, listened to the owls and was not afraid.

Chapter Ten

I slept peacefully that night. In the morning, my favourite music, the dawn chorus, mingled with my dreams and woke me up. I dreamt more often now, at least I made a point of trying to remember dreams more often. I stood a little bit up a hill. It was a clear day. A roe deer pranced by gaily, then I saw a hawk soar above me, searching for the movement of a mouse or some other creature. I watched him as he stood still in the sky. Zoom, he dropped to the ground like a stone, missed his prey and rose up high in the sky again. A blind rabbit hopped by, his eyes stuck closed. That poor creature in pain, by the man introduced disease used to reduce the rabbit population, Myxomatosis. I knew he'd suffer far worse pain and I'd heard you ought to kill these sick bunnies. The thought of crushing its skull with my hoof--horrified me and I left it alone and walked off to try and find something cheerier. It obviously wasn't going to be my day for the next thing I found was a dead pony. I thought I was well into the woods, but instead I came out at a side road. There, by the side of the road, was a brown mare. The crash much have happened in the night, before I left the Mathiesons. Glass covered the road, but there was no sign of the car. I felt sick. Things like that make me weak inside. I began to think that maybe for every bit of happiness you have, you must have a bit of sadness. Could that be the reason for so much suffering? Did everything have to be an even balance?

I walked off again and returned to the woods where I found a warm patch of grass by a pool and lay down comfortably. I wondered what was happening at the stable. Quite some time later, I found out.

Apparently Mr. Harper had been furious when he found I was missing. He would not believe Mrs. Mathieson. He said she was just doing this to him because she'd changed her mind. She called the Police to report me missing, then, ignoring Harper, went out to the stable. She didn't care about Harper now, for he'd been rude to her. She did care about me, though. Never for one moment did she suspect Kevin. As far as she knew, no-one but herself knew about the deal with the American.

Kevin found Ann in a panic.

"Do you know what's happened to Anzor?" she said. "Has he gone already, Kevin."

"No, Ann. I took him into the Forest last night and set him free."

"What?"

"Yes, it's true. I didn't want him to go to America either."

"Where is he now. Do you know?"

"I haven't a clue. I just hope he doesn't come trotting in here for at least another day or two."

"Why, this is wonderful! Kevin you're a genius. I'd never have dared." She was tempted to hug him, but knew he'd rather she didn't so she restrained herself.

"For heavens' sake act innocent, right?" commanded Kevin. "Don't you ever let on what happened, or I'll never be allowed back. Promise me, Ann."

"Okay, I do."

"No, say it. Please say it properly."

"Okay, okay. Kevin, I promise you that I will never tell anyone, without your permission, what has happened to Anzor."

"Why the 'my permission' bit? Who do you want to tell?"

"No-one right now. What if he doesn't come back though? We're going to need help then and I know a girl who has a horse. She'd help us find him and never tell."

"Who?"

"Lindy Dalford."

"Oh, yeah, she's okay. You're not to tell her yet though. Understand?" Kevin threatened.

"Yes, and thanks Kevin. I do appreciate this more than I can say."

Word for word Ann later told me all this. Before I saw Ann again, I was to have even more of an adventure. I just about did cross the sea, only not to the States. More about that later.

My second day in the forest was wonderful. I met a group of five ponies who readily accepted me into their group. They were interested to hear about captive life, for all of them had always been free. I told them the bad and the good side of civilization. They were happy free. We wondered around in our little gang. Twice we bumped into picnickers. Both lots took our photo. We never let them come near enough to touch us though. They tried to tempt us with bread. One of the ponies I was with was very amusing to watch. He loved bread so would approach cautiously and then just as he reached the person, he'd snort and rear. They'd nearly always get such a fright that they'd leap back, dropping the bread. The pony whipped up the bread, ran back to the group and ate it, laughing to himself. Usually the holidaymakers laughed too, realising it had been a trick.

Later in the afternoon, we came across a foal who'd hurt his leg badly. He couldn't stand up for the pain. His mother stood over, licking him. She could not help him. I had never been ill, but I realised then that that is one advantage of living in captivity, at least you have someone to share the responsibilities, such as looking after your foal. At the same time however, it's that very person who will separate you from your offspring when it's about a year old. I couldn't just leave them there and standing looking would do no good. I decided to go and fetch help. Surely any human would call a vet. I hoped so. I left the others and set off briskly in search of a human.

In only fifteen minutes I found a boy of about fourteen with binoculars round his neck and a small rucksack on his back. He was on his own. I whinnied, he approached me. Every step he took, I took one back. We played a similar sort of game for nearly half an hour before we reached the mare and foal. The mare panicked but I quietened her. The boy understood that the foal needed help. He stroked it gently, examined its leg, left his pack and binoculars then ran off carrying a knife. He marked trees along his way to help find his way back. I waited with the mare for what seemed ages, before the boy returned with two men. One carried a gun. The man without the gun examined the foal and then stood up, shaking his head.

"I'm afraid it's broken, John."

"Aye, that's a shame, a mighty shame."

"Better get it over with. Boy, shoo the mare round behind us. Hey, look at that John. Is that not Mathieson's horse, the one that's reported stolen?"

"That's the one that led me here," blurted out the boy, as he ushered the mare to the other side of her foal.

"Right, we'll see to it next. He won't go far, even after the shot. If he's waited here this long, he's not going to desert the mare now."

"Can you not save the foal?" pleaded the boy.

"We would if we could, son. It's some break that. He must have had brittle bones," excused the vet.

John aimed the gun. The boy, not realizing John's hand was already on the trigger, pleaded.

"Wait. Let's take him back. Please." As he said "Please" he grabbed John's shoulder. At the same time, the gun went off. John was swung round by the boy.

The pain screamed into my leg. My first thought was "I'm going to die." I lunged forward and then in a frenzy careered through the woods, the bullet still lodged in my leg. I didn't get far, for the pain slowed me down. I stopped and half leaned against a tree. I stayed there for hours, the blood oozing out, my mind a complete fuzz. I was scared. Petrified.

Late that night I heard a noise of ponies fighting something. I had to see what it was. I limped stiffly forward, opening my wound again, leaving a slim trail of blood. There in the clearing, I saw two men with a large van trying to get a pony up the ramp. One pony was already in, fighting and kicking. Lights appeared on the nearby road. One man ran in the van and tied a twich round the horse's nose. The rope right round his nose, the horse could not even breathe, let alone scream. I was flabbergasted. What could I do? By using the twich, they managed to board the second pony. I suddenly realized who it was. It was the pony who played the game to get bread. The pony I had spent half my day with. I let out a whinny before I realized my mistake. The biggest man came towards me. I turned to flee, but fell. In fear I had forgotten my pain. Before I knew what was happening, I was being hauled into the truck. If I fought, he whipped my leg, I had to give in. The five of us set off. The rough track leading to the road was agony for me. The two others were in mental hysterics. My physical pain was all I could think of. I did not even wonder where we were going. If I had known, my blood would have run cold. A car lit up the road as we turned onto it. From then on it was black, pitch black.

Chapter Eleven

We travelled the whole night and part of the next morning. We were so dehydrated that we looked quite thin. We hobbled out exhausted into a dismal yard. I could smell salt in the air. I did not know that that was the smell of the sea, for I had never seen the sea. The three of us were tied to rings in the wall and given a bucket of water. I was so thirsty that I finished the whole bucket and half of the one next to me, for the bread trick pony didn't want too much. We were given a feed of oats and bran. I gobbled this up and then drank another half bucket of water. My senses were not all there, I doubt.

Another funny looking truck arrived. They did not use the type of boxes normally used to move horses around in. It parked and three New Forest mares were led out.

"Oy, Bert. This was a good idea of yours. Easy as cake, lassoed our three in under an 'alf hour. How d'you get on?"

"Fine. Now belt up will you, we ain't in France yet."

The new man went inside.

"You should've told 'im about the car seeing us leave the clearing," said the other man to Bert.

"Are you kidding? Why worry him? He might back out and leave it all to us."

"France," I thought, "France? Why France?"

Soon the pains began. With my leg in agony, the pains in my stomach were unbearable. Sharp acute pains at first, then just agony. I couldn't even say where. I felt like I was going to die.

I rolled onto the ground and moaned. Bert looked worried.

"Shut up, horse."

Jake and Tom came out to see what the groaning was.

"Looks like colic," said Jake. "You need a vet for that."

"Better just to shoot him. We don't want any vets here."

"Come on, who's going to even guess these are stolen horses?"

"Why shouldn't they? Look at that chestnut's leg. What happened there?" Tom asked as he bent down.

"Cut it, I suppose," answered Bert.

"You beasts, Is this how you catch your horses, shoot them in the leg?"

"What are you on about? That's no bullet wound."

"Have a look."

"Well, so it is. Just as well you noticed. We'd hardly have done it ourselves now would we. The French Authorities would be most puzzled as to how it got there. Get it out. Now."

What does a horse do when he's lying praying he's not dying? Pain all over, I could do no more than groan. I thought of Kevin, how he'd been trying to do me a favour by setting me free. I thought of the foal I'd tried to help, whose bullet was now being torn mercilessly out of my leg. I thought of the pain and how impossible it was to describe. Then one of the men gave me a shot of something. I don't know what he doped me with, but I remember also having something poured down my throat. Then I'd blankets on me and I don't remember any more that day or night, except for waking up once. It had been dark, so now it must be the next day. The worst of the pain was over. I felt very hot.

Apparently, Tom had treated me. I heard them talking as they knocked back beer in the little hut.

"Right, we'll change the chestnut's colour. It's too outstanding and someone might recognise him along with that and the bullet wound. The other five can go on the six o'clock boat tonight and then in a few days, they'll safely be being served up as someone's lunch. I don't foresee any problems. We'll ship them on as our own horses, ready for the knackers, collect the money from Pierre and leave it to him. The chestnut, if he's better, can go tonight, too."

The men dyed my beautiful coat black. I felt horrible. Even my socks and blaze were dyed. The Forest ponies were tied up alongside me in the partially covered yard.

"You asked me about captivity a few days ago. How does it feel?"

"Oh, Anzor, don't talk so, my body feels dead already. I cannot move. My senses have gone. I only plead for a speedy death. How you are still alive, I don't know."

"Nor do I. Maybe it's because no matter how bad I feel, I refuse to accept the fact that I may be actually on my way to the Paradise Star."

"What Paradise Star?"

"Oh, nothing, just a dream I had. A dream that felt real. A place where all the bad things can't get to. They turn into insects without wings and are eaten by the good creatures who can fly to the planet. It was just a dream, but I like dreams."

"It sounds a good dream, Anzor. I too have dreamt of a far off place. Only the creatures didn't have wings, they just floated there, almost invisible. The evil creatures couldn't escape far from their dead bodies. They were attached by a black cord forever and yet could not die. I don't understand that dream, yet it too, was not like a dream. Perhaps one day I will understand it. I hope so. You're right, Anzor, we must not give up hope. Let us plan to escape."

"Bread," as I called him, and I, planned to wait until we were untied, then kick the men and try and kick the yard door down. The four others agreed it was a good plan.

We were untied not long after and led to the same ghastly dirty vans. Only three of us were untied, but we made a break. We freed ourselves of the men, kicked them and ran for the yard door. It was strong, we couldn't kick it open. One man got amidst us. He fell to the ground with a bleeding head and I hoped a broken hand. We kept on kicking and would not give up. Three of us now and two of them. We were ready to attack when the door opened and four more rough types appeared.

"Any trouble, mate?" asked one.

"Get those horses?"

Between the six of them they got us tied up again, only inside the van. I have never known such strong men.

"There's still a chance at the other end," I said to Bread. "Keep hoping."

We were unloaded by the sea. I had never seen so much water. It was lovely. Even feeling as I did, I felt a tingle of excitement for the sea, as I listened to the gulls screeching overhead. Death lay across the water. We only had a little time left. We had been put straight into a pen, thus had had no chance to struggle.

We were not the only ponies. There were many more. Surely, yes it was, there was the big skewbald who had not spoken to me at the dealers. He was too far away to call, so I didn't bother. If my leg had not been bad, I should certainly have tried to jump out. Rather die leaping out of, then stepping into, the grave.

Bread said, "I'm going to jump, Anzor, hope for me, please."

He made it and clattered up the road.

The other pony said, "I'll try too. Hope for me Anzor, hope with all your might."

I hoped but the pony fell, toppled in a heap, broke his neck and died instantly. I hoped for him even then. I hoped he reached the Paradise Star. I believe he did, for he lay there some time before being moved. I could hardly look at the body at first, then I saw all his pain had gone. He even looked happy. So close to my own death, it was necessary for me to believe then, more than any other time, that there was something more, beyond Life.

Eventually the Police came. I saw one of them point to the van.

"Earnest, check your list of registrations. That van brought ponies with spirit. They're not the type that should be going to the knackers."

"Not on the stolen van's list, Eric. Hey, yes, you're right. This is the van reported seen leaving the New Forest. A suspect case, it's listed as."

Earnest got onto his radio and called a patrol car. The men were away catching Bread. They didn't even know about the dead pony yet. The police took me out of the pen. One of them, very observantly, noticed where a little dye had run down over my hoof. That settled matters. They moved me up to a shed. I was later joined by the three Forest mares who came in the van after ours. Nothing happened for about an hour, then Bread joined us. He told us the men had all been arrested without a struggle. He'd heard it said there'd been a good stiff sentence waiting for them, from the Court. I hoped so. I sincerely hoped so. I wished I could have killed them myself. Yet I knew I couldn't kill. "How would I punish them?" I wondered. I fell asleep wondering. I still don't know.

I discovered later how the Police knew I was in the van. The car that had seen the van took note of the number and the clearing it came out of. The clearing was investigated the next day. My trail of blood, and the report of the shooting added up to the conclusion that I'd been stolen. The registration number of the van was circulated to the Police over the country.

The next morning a vet came to see us. He cleaned out my leg as best he could. Some of the dye had got into the wound and horrible yellow stuff was oozing out. His girl assistant washed off the dye round the bad area, then the vet squirted some purple stuff over it. We were still all very nervous as none of us knew what was to become of us. These people seemed friendly though.

We soon got put into a horse float and began a long, tiresome journey.

I had been taken in first. I was glad Bread had been placed next to me.

"Do you think we're going home?" he asked.

"I do. I am sure of it, for I feel at ease."

"I do hope so, Anzor. I am so tired."

"Me, too."

We dozed and nibbled at the hay left for us.

"I shall never feel safe in the Forest again," I heard one of the three mares say. I interrupted.

"Excuse me, but I wouldn't worry. Surely now these men have been caught this will be a lesson to others. They would never have caught you if you hadn't been so busy eating those oats they left down."

"How were we to know it was a trap?"

"Have you ever found oats before?"

"No."

"Then you'll know next time, it's a trap."

"Okay, you're right I hope. Thank you. Now you've made me think about it, I feel better."

"So do we," chorused the other two.

We reached the Mathieson's all in one piece. There was quite a welcoming party, including Ann and Kevin looking very anxious. The Forest ponies were scared of the loose boxes so were turned into a field and fed. I was looked at, cuddled and patted until I felt quite happy. I thankfully went into the box, deep with straw, enjoyed a hot bran mash and fell into the soundest sleep I'd ever had.

Chapter Twelve

The next two months were bliss. Bread and the others had been freed the same day they'd arrived. I had to rest for a long period until my leg got better. I was turned into my favourite field, the one with all the trees in it. One side was alongside the river, another to the road, the third adjoined the Forest, while most of the fourth side looked onto the stable yard. I could never be bored and there was a quiet corner for when I wanted to feel on my own.

Ann visited each day. She was sometimes allowed to take me for a short walk. On one of these jaunts we met Bread. He was well settled and looked in top condition.

Ann recognised Bread and sat down to let me talk with him.

"You are looking well," I told him.

"I feel well. Remember the shy little mare with the white patch and sock? The one next to me in the van?"

"Of course. How could I forget?"

"I look after her now. She's so timid, it's really rather fun."

"Where is she?"

"Oh, she won't come near the roads. I've left her with some others, about five miles from here. I've just come down to tease any picnickers. This'll surely be one of the last hot days of summer. What about you, Anzor? You look content, but haven't you put on rather too much weight?"

"Well,,, I hadn't noticed actually, but now you mention it, I suppose I have. You see I can't go fast any more. I limp as soon as I start trotting. I haven't been ridden since I hurt my leg. I heard the vet say it should be better, but I can't help the limping."

"You're just enjoying a lazy life, I bet. Don't you canter around at night when you're on your own?"

"Bread! Of course not."

"Sorry, Anzor. If the vet says there's no reason for you to limp then I hope he's right. Have you really wanted to go back to being ridden by all those children and adults, for hours every day? I don't blame you if you're enjoying a rest. I'd hate it, having people you'd never seen spoken to your back and pulling at your mouth."

"It's not always like that. I have had some super times."

"Why don't you break out? Come and join our herd. You'd be most welcome."

"No, I couldn't do that. I know I'd be caught. Perhaps if I caused the Mathiesons any more trouble they'd sell me. There are many horrible stables, Bread, places where you stand on your own dirt for a week at a time. There are stables where the doors don't fit and draughts come blowing in through the cracks. Or it can be the other way round, a dark dingy stable with no fresh air at all. You feel as though you could choke on the stale air. No Bread, I have it good at this stable. These people like horses. I have been kept by people who didn't care if I lived or died. I was just a horse to be trained to obey at their slightest command. I was supposed to be like a well-behaved robot, automatic and with no mind. I like it the way things are."

"Especially on holiday," added Bread. "I don't mean to interfere, Anzor, but why do the Mathiesons keep you now? You're no use to them lame, just eating up their grass."

"Bread, don't say these things. I couldn't bare to be sold. Please stop."

"I'm only thinking of you, Anzor. It's time you exercised your leg more. I've often been lame. Unless you get exercise, your leg will got so stiff that it really will hurt to move. Goodbye, Good luck, I hope I see you soon."

He tossed his mane and trotted off.

Ann pulled my rope, encouraging me on. I refused and turned back. I wanted to think. Bread had really upset me.

We arrived back at the stable and were met by Mrs. Mathieson, looking very serious.

"How is he, Ann?"

"He wouldn't go on today. He made me take him home."

"Ann, I know how fond of Anzor you are, but I've decided not to keep him. He is of no use here as long as he can't be ridden. I'm fond of him too, I've waited two months. The vet said three weeks should have put him back to normal."

I could feel Ann trembling, or perhaps it was me.

"Who would buy him?" she asked.

"There's a home for handicapped children only ten miles away. Anzor could go there. They have one pony who is more of a pet, but can be ridden by some of the children. They want a bigger pony as well. They only walk with these children on their backs to help give them confidence. He'll be treated well."

"When?" was all Ann said.

"I have to go and see them yet. There's no great rush. I'm really thinking of winter. It costs a lot to feed a horse then. However, I may as well get him in at his new home as soon as possible, in case they get another offer."

"How much do you want for him?"

"That's hardly your business, Ann. Now run along. I'll see to Anzor."

"No, I mean, I may buy him."

"But Ann, he can't be ridden."

"I don't care. I love him. I need him."

"It wouldn't be fair on you, Ann. If your parents get you a pony, get a healthy one."

End of conversation. What was I going to do? Funny, Bread was dead right. He really is clever, especially for a wild horse.

A lot went on in Ann's house that night, as I found out from her the next day. She went home, shedding buckets of tears.

"Whatever has happened, dear?" asked her mother.

"Anzor's being sold, mum. Oh, mum, please, please can't we buy him, mum, please. He's going cheap, because of his leg. He won't cost us much, mum. I'll even do my homework for an hour every night. I'll be so grateful. You won't need to do anything for him. I'll look after him so well."

Dad appeared. "What's this, Ann? Anzor's being sold?"

"Yes, oh yes, dad, please think about it. Don't just say no."

"Now don't build up your hopes, Ann, but your mother and I have been discussing the possibility of getting you a pony. In fact only last night we phoned up Lindy's aunt to see what they'd charge for keeping one with Blue."

"Dad, I can't believe it."

"Wait, Ann. I'm not finished yet. The actual stabling we could afford, at a push, but there's a saddle, bridle, shoes, vets bills. There are never-ending expenses with a horse. Ann, we can't afford to take a chance on a cripple."

"I don't want any horse. If I can't have the horse I love, then it would be very unfaithful to take another one. No, dad, mum. Thank you, but no. If you believe in me, then believe that Anzor will get better. I believe it."

Meanwhile I was thinking over what Bread had said. He was right, I had become lazy. The slightest bit of stiffness and I'd limped, not seeing any need to exert myself. The pain had not been bad for weeks. Thinking is all very well, but it's action that gets you places. If Bread had not been honest, I would probably never have realised what I hoped was to be the truth.

Waiting until dusk seemed sensible. When night reached out to shade us from the sun, I began my trial. Walking round the field was easy. How trotting, oh, it did hurt, perhaps I was to be lame for life. I rested and tried again and continued resting and trotting until the moon was high in the sky. By then I was so tired that I could hardly tell if my leg was sore or not, it certainly wasn't very bad.

Early next morning, off again. I snorted in glee, I could trot. I had just been stiff. Whinneying, I broke into a canter, but in doing so the pain came back. Of course, I use different muscles for cantering, I hadn't yet strengthened or stretched them. I'd try again later.

A car turned up the drive and stopped at the house. Ann jumped out. The man who followed was tall and fair. I recognised him as Ann's dad. They were met at the door by Mrs. Mathiesons, who invited them in.

Some time later, a girl with a smile as big as a banana came rushing over to me, not realising how anxious I was to know what on Earth was going on. I stamped my foot to give her the message.

"Anzor, Anzor, you're mine, really and truly mine."

I never learnt why her father had changed his mind. I suppose a happy daughter leads to a peaceful home life. He certainly had made me a happy horse.

Chapter Thirteen

Blue was given the pleasure of my company for the second time in his life. Ann led me to the gate accompanied by Lindy. They stood and watched, hopeful that history would not repeat itself. It didn't.

Blue snorted, "You're here to stay, are you?"

"Yes, I am. You know you have the power to get me removed. Do you intend to throw me out again?"

"Of course not. You're not a silly little colt now, are you?"

"I wasn't silly then."

"Yes, you were."

"I was not."

"Why did you trot around whinnying then?" It was enough to get on anyone's nerves, especially one used to a peaceful life."

"Blue, I had left my mother for the first time that same day. I was lonely."

"There, I told you you were silly, you've just admitted that it was because you were lonely."

"I refuse to argue. I was not silly. The cause of my loneliness was leaving my mother and you being the only horse around, I naturally approached you for company. To this day it seemed the sensible thing to do."

"Okay, Anzor. I was only testing you to see if you had a strong enough character to stick up for yourself. You see, I've no time for weaklings. Make yourself at home. I've been here a year, you'll like it."

"Thank you, Blue."

We looked over towards the girls who were obviously pleased with Blue and me. They ran up to Aunt Joan's farmhouse laughing.

That night I did not exercise my leg. The next day, I tried trotting but felt pain again. I swore then that I would practise last thing at night and each morning until I could surprise Ann with my recovery.

Three weeks passed and I was able to canter for a short time. The weather had been dull, but Saturday dawned fair. Lindy was not even up when Ann called me from the gate. She had recently taken to riding me, though only at a walk.

Slipping on my bridge and saddle, Ann mounted and turned me towards the village. On and on we walked. There's one thing about walking, it gives you so much more time to look around. The leaves were purple, brown, green and auburn. They drifted, flying, floating and flopping to the ground. Released at last from the branch that had held them for so long, the leaves tumbled joyfully in their new found freedom, ending in death on the forest floor. Surely they're not dead, I thought, only serving a different purpose in life. From leaves, to multi-coloured carpets for me to trot over, or for a hedgehog to hibernate in. My thoughts were then interrupted by Ann urging me on.

"Come on, Anzor. How about trying a little trot? Just a little trot. Try."

I not only tried but trotted smoothly with almost no effort. Need I say how delighted my affectionate owner was.

"Anzor, you rascal. You are wonderful. I can hardly wait to tell dad."

We came to a pool and rested there for almost an hour, before heading home a shorter way than we had come.

We had not gone far when I smelt smoke. Ann stood up in her stirrups to try and see where it was coming from. We trotted quickly round the corner and there in the trees was a beautiful cottage, smoke pouring from the upstairs window.

"It's Mrs. Leeron's cottage, Anzor. Quickly. Come on."

She threw herself off me and ran to the door, bursting through it. A fat Dalmatian leapt out whining and cowered by the bare rhododendron bush. Ann soon came down the stairs, half carrying a white-haired old lady. She dragged out a rug and put it round the woman whom she'd sat in the garden chair. Mrs. Leeron coughed and took a deep breathe. The sparsely spotted dog lay at her feet, licking her leg. Seeing that the women had come too. Ann rushed inside and I saw her carry a bucket of water upstairs.

Soon she rushed down.

"It's no use, Anzor. We need help. Take this quickly to anyone. Go on, Anzor, get help."

She screamed at me as she pushed the notes she'd written, one on to my saddle and one on my bridle.

I was scared of the flames, obviously beyond her control. My fear was heightened by Ann's panicky screams and the dog's howling. I took off from a standstill to a gallop and hustled off the path onto the road that led back to the village. I kept on the grass verge until a car came. Controlling my fear, shaking, I stood on the road. The car drove past me as if I wasn't there. Now anger was stronger than terror as I galloped to the village. All the people stopped to look at me but at first no-one approached me as I stood pawing the ground. At last an old farmer took my reins, and the notes.

"It's okay, he's quiet now. I haven't got my glasses though, can anyone tell me what this says?"

"By now a good crowd had gathered. How they wasted time. A young woman read the plea for help and then action started. Somebody who recognised me offered to take me home. I heard someone else say, "I thought that was a lame horse."

Everyone else rushed off and soon the fire engine, siren blasting the peace, followed by at least ten cars, headed for the burning cottage.

Curiosity overcame the man holding me. Instead of taking me to the farm, he walked towards the fire.

By the time we arrived, the fire was out. An ambulance had just driven off with Mrs. Leeron, who was suffering from shock. The top floor of the small cottage was badly burnt, leaving a hole in the roof. Ann was shaking she was now the centre of attention, the heroine who that night got her photo in the local paper. I never saw the photo, but I did hear that I, too, was in it.

Ann was taken home by car. She took the Dalmatian with her, having offered to care for it until the old lady recovered.

Boy, did I deserve a good feed that night. Thank goodness I got one, for by the time I got home I felt like I'd been out for two weeks instead of one long day.

Little did I know how that day was going to change my life.

Chapter Fourteen

The change happened like this. Old Mrs. Leeron had not suffered too badly. She had nowhere to stay until her house was repaired. Being an old friend of Aunt Joan's now dead mother, the Aunt felt obliged to ask her to stay, especially as Lindy had already taken in the dog, who was not only fat, but pregnant. Ann's mother had not let her keep her.

Mrs. Leeron's husband had been very rich, but when he died, she felt the need to return to a simpler life. Not needing much space, she had moved to the cottage, from her big house and had lived there the last fifteen years. This cottage was the very one she had lived in as a little girl.

The puppies were born, all thirteen of them. One died, leaving twelve hungry puppies, anxious to get at their mother's milk. Ann was so busy helping Lindy with those puppies, she hardly had any time for me. It wasn't her fault, for Aunt Joan had the farm to look after. Mrs. Leeron was still recovering, or so she said. She actually spent half her time with me, teaching me all sorts of tricks. Had she really run off to join a circus when she was twelve? So she told Ann.

She had me pawing the ground seven times if she said seven, acting dead if she shot me with a toy gun. I loved the attention. It was great fun, especially as I always got an apple to finish with.

Poor jealous Blue. Mrs. Leeron had tried to work with him. It had been really funny. Blue just stood looking at her as if she was completely off her head. Blue had no fun in him at all.

She said "Two" and tapped her long stick twice on the ground. She repeated this many times, then tapping Blue's leg twice instead of the ground.

Blue ignored her, yawned and pretended to fall asleep.

Mrs. Leeron scratched her head and came to me. Having watched it all with Blue I already knew exactly what I had to do. I chuckled as she praised me, eager to learn more.

Every day from then on I was trained for either a complete morning or afternoon. Ann rode me most days now and I was getting back to my old fit self. Ann was always a bit lazy with the grooming, but Mrs. Leeron would brush me for hours. She didn't seem like an old woman. In fact I swear she'd more energy than Lindy and Ann put together.

Now that winter had come, Blue and I were indoors. We had one end of a cow shed partitioned off. There were some goats at the other end, and usually the odd hen clucking around. With all this and cows in the next shed it was a noisy place.

The puppies had grown into chubby playful pups. They were seven weeks old the first time they tumbled into the barn.

"Oh, Blue, look at Princess's puppies."

"I can see them. Silly creatures."

I might have known that Blue would have said that.

They yapped and ran under the bar. I lowered my head to sniff them. As they tried to clamber up my head, I quickly withdrew it. They were all around us, jumping, yelping, rolling, all except one who sat outside whimpering with a paw raised. Suddenly Blue lifted up his leg and stamped his hoof down. Ten puppies ran out to the yard. The one with the sore paw looked. The one under Blue, gulped and died.

"I didn't mean to kill it," he whispered. "I only meant to scare them. Get rid of them."

I whinnied and whinnied as loudly as I could until Lindy appeared, quickly followed by Ann and Aunt Joan.

Blue showed his guilt by standing with head down, the guilty hoof resting lightly on its toe, wishing it had never been raised. The girls cried and Ann picked up the puppy onlooker who seemed too stunned to move. The dead bundle was removed sadly, by Aunt Joan, whose tears would never bring it back to life. I wanted out. I couldn't bear to stay there where death had visited so recently.

No-One freed me. Ann left with the puppy, never looking back.

"Anzor, can you ever forgive me?" a humble voice asked.

"Blue, you say it was an accident. I believe it was in a way, but deep in your mind, deep inside you, you wanted one to die, I feel sure. You hate young, innocent creatures. Why?"

"I was never allowed such fun as a foal. My mother died as I was born. I was fed milk by a mare whose foal had died. She let me drink from her, but never cared for me at all. Our home was a filthy shed in a small muddy field, too small to really stretch my legs in. We belonged to a heartless couple who bred a few horses and dogs. They cared for the dogs, but never spoke to us as other than dumb creatures. I hated living as soon as I was born. No-one bought me and I stayed there for four years, broken in by the same couple. The man got on my back and stuck there like a wasp in jam. I tried everything to get him off. He whipped and whipped me till I didn't care how long he sat on me. If ever I showed any spirit, I was beaten till weak. Lindy bought me out of pity and has trained me how to behave with her. Apart from that, I don't know much about life. You're the only other horse I've ever spoken to, Anzor. I am bitter, Anzor. I thought I had reason to be. Now though, now that I've taken a life just begun, I realise how wrong I have been. All these years I've wasted. All my thoughts were of the past. I never thought of the future or of anyone else's future. I only ever felt sorry for myself. I've learnt my lesson. I am really going to try to help others. I'll even let Mrs. Leeron train me if it makes her happy. I won't bite Lindy when she tightens my girths. Yes, Anzor, I'm going to be a new horse. I'll think of now and tomorrow. How good things are. No more yesterdays for me. Will you believe me, Anzor?"

"Blue, you have made a sad day into a happy day. The puppy's death was not in vain if you have really learnt such a lesson from it. We shall see, Blue. We shall see."

Chapter Fifteen

The puppy whom Ann had taken in was given to her as a present. She called him "Jody." He had lots of spots and looked much better than his mother. The rest of the puppies were sold. Jody would never go near Blue, but soon became used to me and would run around me, yapping and biting at my legs. He was very annoying, actually, but I couldn't think how to stop him without hurting him. Fortunately, one day as he yelped at my legs, I side-stepped and stood on his tail. He howled and took off to the barn, tail between legs, looking for his beloved mistress who was feeding the hens with her friend. From then on Jody and I had a much better relationship. He still played with me, but never bit my legs again.

The grand day came when Mrs. Leeron asked Ann's parents, Aunt Joan and the girls to come and see my performance. Kevin, whom I hadn't seen for a while, also appeared that day. He had been given one of the puppies for Christmas and was soon to make a habit of visiting to let the puppies play or in the hope of being offered a ride on me or Blue.

His pup was called Domino.

Mrs. Leeron had plaited my mane with yellow ribbons. I wore a yellow bow in my tail and a yellow halter she had bought and dyed for me. We had gone over the routine so many times that I knew it easily. I bowed to the onlookers, then caught the sugar lump reward offered me. Then I had to pretend I was in school. I was asked to paw the ground to give the answers to easy sums. Of course, I couldn't really add, but I did know that every time Mrs. Leeron waggled her little finger, she wanted me to paw the ground. No-one but myself noticed the very slight movement made on her hand. Next I trotted round, doing a floating extended trot, turned a circle and came back to receive a carrot. My last trick had been my most difficult. It had been three weeks before I had realised that when she shot me with her toy gun, I was to lie down. My reward for this encouraged me to make such an effort. The small crowd were delighted and clapped heartily, then they all went in for tea, cakes and lemonade, hastily followed by Jody, whom I had noticed always followed to where there was food. He was a real greedy guts.

Mrs. Leeron apparently was delighted to find that she could still train horses. When she had married, her circus life had been put behind her as a happy memory. Now her ambitions were raised. She returned to her cottage and said to everyone that she'd have a surprise for them if they'd leave her for a few months.

"Come on April Fools Day," she called as she climbed into Aunt Joan's old car. As it turned out, she came for the day every Sunday after that, but still the surprise at her home was put off until April.

Except for the exciting day of the drag hunt, life became very quiet after the old lady left. The hunt was held five miles away. Blue and I were brushed thoroughly, while it was still dark.

"Come on, Ann, it's time we were going," called Lindy to Ann who was combing her hair.

"I'm ready Lindy. Isn't this exciting? Don't forget we have to wait for Kevin."

"Oh, I am glad you remembered. I had completely forgotten. Did you say he was hiring Frisky?"

"Of course. He hardly ever rides anybody else."

"That's him now, I can hear a horse."

Before the girls reached the door, a bedraggled looking boy put his head round it."

"Cor. It's bucketing," he said.

"Oh, no. I didn't realise it was so heavy. We'll get soaked."

"If we don't go, we'll always regret it. Let's leave right now," suggested Ann.

Off we trotted in the pouring rain. By the time we got to the hotel from where the hunt left I could feel Ann's feet squelching in her riding boots. No-one looked very happy. However, we were lucky and the rain storm passed, leaving a dull, but dry, sky. In a drag hunt, the trail is left by a scent of aniseed. The hounds follow this with as much speed and noise as if chasing a fox. They are given a reward of meat when they reach the end of the trail. This way the course can be chosen and of course no fox is involved. I had heard tales of real hunts which seemed so ridiculous, all those people chasing one poor little fox. I was very glad this was a drag hunt.

Blue, true to his word, had cheered up over the last few weeks. He was looking forward to this day out. There were about forty to fifty horses and ponies, all keen to be off. Soon the hunt began, once everyone had said all their "hellos" and "how do you do's?".

We were near the front and kept up very well. Blue and I lost sight of each other when we had to queue up for a jump. Kevin and Frisky tore on ahead of us. There were all sorts of jumps, ditches, hedges, streams, wooden fences. We managed them all, until I got a loose shoe. We'd had about an hours ride and just as I landed after jumping a wall, I felt my shoe slide. I stopped immediately, in fact so suddenly that Ann almost went flying over my head. If I'd been feeling naughty, I would probably have put my head down to help her on her way.

She was very angry about the shoe, and tried to get it off. It was stuck half on, half off, and would not move.

"Oh, well, there's nothing for it but to go to see Mr. Smith," she said. Mr. Smith was, as his name suggested, the local blacksmith.

We crossed the fields and entered the woods.

Ann said to herself, "I wonder if we could cut through the hunt-master's grounds. I know all his family will be out at the hunt, they always are."

She decided to do so. We crossed the woods and went through a little iron gate. The grounds were fairly big, but only had a small lawn. The surrounds were all woodland left to grow naturally. It was through these trees we walked. Suddenly Ann froze, I looked up and could see why. There, coming out of a downstairs window, was a small man carrying a large briefcase. He looked around, but didn't see us as he ran into the woods ahead of us. Ann let go of me and followed the man as silently as I tried to follow her. He never looked back, he was so intent on getting out of the grounds. The little man with a black moustache climbed over the fence. I think he saw me then but I'm not sure. Ann was well hidden though. She climbed the fence after him, leaving me all alone. I wasn't sure what to do. I suppose she knew that with my loose shoe I wouldn't want to travel far. But I couldn't just stand there. I watched them climb down the hill and head for the road, before they disappeared out of sight.

Realising I'd wasted too much time, I cantered across the lawn and out of the front gate. I headed down the road and slowed down to cautiously turn the corner. There I saw the thief jump into a big car and drive off. He didn't see me this time. When he turned the next corner I noticed Ann retracing her steps and whinnied to let her know I was here. She ran up to me, jumped on and we were off, following the car. Luckily my shoe fell off very soon. Of course, we didn't catch up on the car, but when we got to the next village about four miles from where the break in had taken place. we were more than lucky to see that same car parked outside a pub.

"At least I've got his number this time," I heard Ann murmur. "What if I forget it?"

Even before Ann dismounted, the thief, revived by his pint of ale, was all set to drive to safety. Ann jumped off me and interrupted him. There was no-one else around.

"Excuse me," said Ann. "Can you help me? I'm looking for View Street."

I suppose she was trying to fill in time until someone else appeared to help her.

"No, I'm not from here. Sorry, dear," he said very politely.

"Do you think you could ask in the pub for me?"

"No, I'm in a hurry. I have a meeting. Excuse me."

"Oh, please, I've been looking for ages."

"Look, little girl, I am a busy man with more important things to do than run messages for children. If you don't stand out of my way I may become very angry. Excuse me, please."

"No, I can't." Ann didn't know what to say. "Anzor, help."

I trotted forward and pushed the man against his car. At that moment, the pub's landlord appeared.

"Get that horse away from me," the thief called.

Ann called the landlord. "Help, please. That man's a thief. Look in his briefcase."

"Now, miss," he replied, "That's a bad thing to say about a man without proof."

"How ridiculous," the thief interrupted. "I could get you into serious trouble for calling me that. Now remove your horse and let me go."

"You're not letting him go are you?" gasped Ann as the thief opened the car door.

"Well, perhaps if I could see your card, sir. Do you have proof of your identity?" The man produced what later proved to be a false business card, but the landlord was satisfied.

"Now, don't you come here again, young lady, annoying my customers, or I'll get the Police onto you."

"I wish you would. He is a thief."

I could tell Ann felt a fool and was near to tears. I had to help her. I lunged at the thief, knocked him down and grabbed the briefcase off the front seat. As my teeth pulled it onto the ground it burst open, revealing the stolen property, jewels and silver cutlery.

The thief ran, but I headed him off until the landlord and Ann grabbed him. By then three men who had been in the pub came out and helped in the struggle. The Police were called and Ann was asked to write a statement. My photo was taken.

"Fame again," I thought and bowed to the photographer as Mrs. Leeron had taught me. He was very amused and everyone laughed.

Ann laughed even more when she got her £100 reward.

Chapter Sixteen

April Fools Day came. All of us who had been at my performance now went to Sunflower Cottage, so called because in summer the cottage was surrounded by those beautiful tall flowers. Mrs. Leeron took us round to the back of her house and we horses were tied to the hedge, which tasted quite good, while the humans sat down. Domino and Jody played with their mother affectionately.

Mrs. Leeron went inside, put on a noisy record and was followed outside by a tiny Shetland pony and five poodles, two white, two black and one brown. Princess, her Dalmatian, joined the group. The dogs all sat on drums while the pony did various tricks far better than I ever managed. The brown poodle then jumped on her back while the other dogs, led by Princess, danced in a line round and round the trotting Shetland. Princess retired from the act while the dogs danced on balls, slid down chutes, swung on swings and did acrobatics. The final act was a game of football, with Tiny the Shetland, ridden by just the brown poodle, against the other four. The poodles scored two goals while Tiny and "Fudge" scored one. The six animals leapt over a couple of jumps on their way out, then were brought over to meet us all.

We were all delighted. Even more so, when Mrs. Leeron admitted to having been asked to do her show for various Charities. She was certainly going to have a busy summer. We all spent the whole day there, enjoying a wonderful buffet lunch. Yes, Blue, Tiny and I were fed sandwiches and cake too. It's not every day you get spoiled. What a super day it was. Six months ago, Blue probably would never have spoken to merry little Tiny. That day, they chatted non-stop. The little mare and Blue remained firm friends forever. Of course, I was friends with her too, but then I always like making friends.

As we ate lunch I heard a whinny. There at the bottom of the large garden, looking over the fence was Bread. Ann quickly took him a cheese sandwich. He didn't back away this time but ate it gratefully. I pulled at my rope until Ann untied me. She gave Bread another sandwich and left us to exchange our news.

"Bread, I haven't seen you for ages. I owe a lot to you. You made me see sense. I'm as healthy as can be now."

"That's great, Anzor, and I have some news for you."

He whinnied and out from behind the bushes appeared the mare he'd befriended, followed by a little foal, the image of Bread.

The mare and foal greeted me politely. They knew I was pleased to see them but would understand when after a few minutes they returned to the safety of the trees, leaving Bread and me to continue our conversation.

After we'd exchanged our months of news, Bread stated, "We've proved one thing, Anzor."

"What?"

"That dreams can come true, just as long as you keep hoping, keep believing in their possibility."

"Yes, we know to give up, in a horse's world, is to die. Yes, Bread, we have made our dreams come true. May your son grow to spread the words of Hope even further."

"Thank you, Anzor, you are a true friend. I'll visit you again soon. Meantime, keep believing and help others to do so, Goodbye, friend."

"Goodbye."

I stood and watched him return to his family, then I turned to mine. I smiled inside. What a big family. Horses, dogs and people, we all made one big happy family. I snorted and walked towards them, Ann ran to greet me and hugged me.

"You make me so happy, Anzor."

Would she ever know how happy she'd made me?

THE END.

CPSIA information can be obtained
at www.ICGtesting.com
Printed in the USA
BVHW031912090120
569115BV00001B/92/P